"My b-a-a-by, my b-a-a-by.
It's too s-o-o-o-n."

Morgan's heart constricted with pity and love for her foster daughter.

"Just work with us here and do as we say. We're all going to help, honey," Morgan instructed her in a calm voice, forcing a reassuring smile. "That's a good girl. Breathe through this contraction. Breathe, breathe...."

"Head's presenting. Next contraction will do it. You've got to push when I say, Tessa," Luke urged.

Tessa's eyes bulged with pain and panic, and Morgan continued to talk quietly into her ear.

"That's it, sweetie. Push. Good girl. Push now, push...."

The entire team joined in the litany, and with deceptive slowness Tessa's daughter was born.

She was alive but impossibly tiny and flaccid. Her vital signs were flat.

Dear Reader,

In the coal-mining valley where I grew up, a girl had two career choices: she could be either a teacher or a nurse. I chose to be a nurse, and I actually went off to nurse's training for all of a week before I realized that although the idea of medicine fascinated me, nursing just wasn't where I belonged.

That early enchantment with the healing arts never faded, however. It made me an avid reader of all things medical...but a little knowledge can be a dangerous thing. When the idea for this series occurred to me, I was elated—here was a chance to create an entire medical dynasty, to perform operations and deliver babies. But then it dawned on me that I wasn't exactly qualified.

That's when my good friends stepped in, many of them involved in medicine. With excitement and enthusiasm and generosity, they answered questions, read parts of the manuscripts and gently corrected both my terminology and my surgical skills.

Then came one of the highlights of my life—a hands-on encounter with birth. My daughter-in-law, bless her generous soul, invited me to be present when my grandson was born. Of course, I'd been there when my own three sons arrived, but somehow I'd been too busy to absorb all the details. Dr. Julia Reynolds guided Laine into the world with such expertise and love, I knew I had to write about an obstetrician. Or maybe two.

I've had the time of my life researching and writing these books. May you have just as much enjoyment reading them.

Love always,

Bobby Hutchinson

THE BABY DOCTOR
Bobby Hutchinson

Harlequin Books

TORONTO • NEW YORK • LONDON
AMSTERDAM • PARIS • SYDNEY • HAMBURG
STOCKHOLM • ATHENS • TOKYO • MILAN
MADRID • WARSAW • BUDAPEST • AUCKLAND

ISBN 0-373-70753-3

THE BABY DOCTOR

For Laine Jackart

Babies are the nicest way to make people

Heartfelt thanks to Monica Adamack; Lynda Knauf and Lynda Greer, obstetrical nurses; Pat Ford, friend and medical advisor; Lois McCloskey, artistic consultant; and most of all, Dr. Greg McCloskey, who treats my patients as though they are his own.

CHAPTER ONE

DR. MORGAN JACOBSEN paused in the vestry of the small old church, breathing hard and brushing raindrops from her new blue dress. The September day had gone from sunny to sodden in the past hour, catching her without a raincoat or an umbrella.

Inside, the congregation was silent, and the pastor's rich voice floated back to her along with the heady scent of bridal flowers and the special subtle aroma of beeswax and holiness that all churches seemed to exude.

"Gathered here today—"

Rats. Morgan's heart sank and she scowled. She was soaking wet, out of breath, and now she was late for Celia's wedding.

As usual, she'd had a last-minute phone call, this one from Joyce Tucker, an expectant mother in her final week of pregnancy.

"Morgan, my mother wants to know if my grandmother can be there when my baby comes." Joyce had sounded stressed, and Morgan hastened to reassure her.

"Sure, Joyce, I've got no objections to that."

But then Joyce had burst into hysterical tears. "Please, please, don't let her come," she sobbed. "I don't want her there. Granny's bossy, she's cranky, she says awful things and she'll spoil everything. It's all Mom's idea to ask her," the girl had wailed.

So Morgan had said that Granny absolutely couldn't be present; Mother, either, if it was upsetting to Joyce. But it had taken time to calm her patient and reassure her that it was a personal decision who should attend the birth of her baby, not a matter of family politics.

She really ought to get a cell phone, Morgan concluded. And she ought to keep an umbrella in the Jeep. She'd been halfway across town before she realized it was starting to pour in typical Vancouver cloudburst fashion. And of course it had been impossible to find a parking space near the church on this busy west-end street. She'd finally abandoned her Jeep in a lot blocks away and gotten soaked during the mad dash to the church.

Now she'd missed watching Celia float up the aisle. It was so maddening, because Morgan loved weddings. Not as much as she loved delivering babies, but weddings came a close second. Like most births, weddings were joyful occasions, even though she'd pretty much given up hope for one of her own.

At thirty-six, she'd had only two serious romances in her entire life, and they'd both ended years ago. She was philosophical about her single state when she had time to think about it at all. What the heck. She was darned lucky, really. She had a career that consumed her, a foster daughter she was growing to love, a home of her own that she adored. And if she could only get where she was going on time, she'd have it made.

Feeling self-conscious, she stepped from the foyer into the church. It was crowded, and there was no sign of the ushers. Morgan did her best to tiptoe silently down the aisle to a pew where she spied a single empty space, but she was wearing the beige pumps that squeaked with every step, and the sound made heads turn.

Several people smiled and waggled their fingers at her. Celia worked in X ray at St. Joseph's Medical Center, Morgan's alma mater, and among the guests were lots of familiar faces from the hospital. Morgan was no longer on staff at St. Joe's—she'd left a year ago to join a small clinic devoted to women's health—but because the clinic used the hospital facilities, she was back regularly, delivering babies and using St. Joe's operating theaters.

Reaching the pew at last, Morgan slid past a man with a huge belly and a woman in a startling yellow hat and settled into the narrow space, aware too late that the man in front of her must be six foot seven, with shoulders that blotted out any view of the bridal party.

Morgan gave a regretful sigh. Well, at least she could hear what was going on.

"—take this man to be your lawfully—"

A manicured finger tapped her shoulder, and she twisted her head and smiled a pleased greeting at the woman seated directly behind her. It was Pam Albright, a nurse from the hospital and now one of Morgan's patients.

Pam gave Morgan a wan smile, shifting her hugely pregnant body back into the cushioning arc of her husband's, Frank's, arm. Pam had been in for her checkup two days before, and Morgan expected her to deliver in about three weeks. Pam and Frank had waited a long time for this baby. They were both in their late thirties, and it was their first. They knew from ultrasound that it was a girl, and Morgan hoped and expected everything would go well for them. So far, the pregnancy had been uneventful.

"—pronounce you husband and wife. You may kiss the bride—"

Morgan craned her neck, but her view was still blocked by the giant in front of her. The organ began to play softly, and the congregation rustled and whispered as the bridal pair went off to the vestry to sign the register. Morgan glanced down at her lap and noticed that the rain had somehow darkened and puckered the blue fabric of her dress, making it look as if it had developed a bizarre skin disease. And there was a brownish stain she couldn't account for near the hem.

She recrossed her legs so the stain didn't show, but a second later the organ music swelled into a rendition of the wedding march and she surged to her feet with the rest of the congregation, wishing for the millionth time that she was taller than five-one. She stood on her toes and craned her neck for a glimpse of the bridal pair.

Suddenly, a sharp cry from the pew behind her made her look around. A single glance at Pam's stricken face made Morgan struggle past the bodies blocking her from the aisle.

"Excuse me, s'cuse me. Let me past, please—"

At last she broke free. Pam's husband, his face ashen, had half lifted his wife into the aisle. Bloodstained fluid was gushing down Pam's legs, pooling on the oak flooring. The membranes had ruptured, and Pam was obviously having violent contractions.

"There's something hanging down—" Pam's anguished whisper alerted Morgan, and oblivious to the craning heads and curious, shocked faces surrounding them, she squatted down and lifted the hem of Pam's long, loose maternity dress.

Holy toot. A bolt of panic went skittering through her. The umbilical cord, the baby's lifeline in the uterus, had prolapsed, slipping into the vaginal canal along with the rush of amniotic fluid. The baby's life was in terrible danger, its vital supply of oxygen already cut off.

Morgan reached up and deftly pulled Pam's underwear down around her ankles, then grabbed her hands and urged her to her knees.

"Down. Get down on your hands and knees, right now, head on your hands, bottom in the air. Frank, help her."

Morgan's voice, deep throated and urgent, rose above the organ music, and when Pam hesitated, Morgan took her upper arms and, with Frank's help, bodily forced her to the floor.

"Hold her there. Don't let her move," she commanded Pam's horrified husband.

He crouched with an arm across his wife's body, stammering, "I don't understand. What's going on? Is the ba-baby coming right now?" His eyes were filled with terror.

"Just keep her down. Keep her still." There

was no time for explanations. Morgan threw herself to her knees behind her patient, searching for the unborn baby's shoulder and lifting it away from the compressed umbilical cord.

Pam's scream of agony rose above the organ music, and there were shocked and appalled exclamations from wedding guests who didn't understand what was going on.

"Someone get an ambulance here fast. This baby's in a hurry to get born." Morgan tried, for Frank's sake, to sound calm and upbeat, but the effort she was exerting made it hard to talk at all. It was absolutely essential she maintain a steady pressure on the baby, pushing her back into Pam's pelvis, preventing the unborn child's weight from cutting off her own oxygen supply. She couldn't release the tension for an instant, not until anesthetic was administered, or the baby would surely die. And the pressure required was utterly agonizing for Pam, as well as for Morgan.

In spite of her years as an obstetrician, Morgan had only seen this condition twice before, and both times it had occurred in the delivery room, with help readily available.

Here, in a church…well, it was going to be touch and go.

"Ambulance is on its way." One of the guests from the hospital had understood all too well the seriousness of the situation and raced back to make the call from the pastor's office.

"Somebody get me some wine, quick." It dawned on Morgan that alcohol might slow or stop the contractions tearing through Pam, who was now alternately moaning and sobbing with pain.

The request was relayed urgently from guest to guest, and it was the pastor in his white robes who finally crouched beside Morgan, proffering an overflowing water glass filled with wine. His hands trembled so hard that some of the dark red liquid normally used for the sacrament sloshed across Morgan's shoulder and trickled slowly down her aching arm.

"Not for me. Give it to her, please." Morgan could smell the spilled wine, like vinegar, pungent even over the animal scent of hot blood and amniotic fluid.

Mighty cheap wine for the sacrament, she thought hysterically. "Drink it down, Pam. Try to swallow some," she begged. "It'll slow the contractions. It'll help us here, honey. Do it. I know this is hard, but you're so brave, you're doing just great. Hang in there, okay? Frank, see if you can get some of that into her."

Morgan could hear Frank pleading as Pam gulped the wine, and she felt the tremors of her patient's body as she tried not to retch. Her shoulder and entire arm began to tremble with the strain, and she wished to goodness someone would tell the organist to either pack it in or play something a bit more upbeat. Even a Sousa march would fit this occasion better than Handel.

The guests who worked at the hospital were grouped around, doing whatever they could to help. A nursing aide in a pink satin dress was kneeling, rubbing Pam's back, and someone else—oh, bless them—was massaging Morgan's shoulders with strong, capable strokes, but it seemed to take an eternity before the ambulance crew finally raced in.

It was a difficult and clumsy procedure to load Pam onto the stretcher, still in the head-down position, with Morgan attached to her like a human lifeline. Luckily, the attendants managed the awkward process with a minimal amount of confusion.

Prolapse required an immediate C-section, and Morgan had the ambulance crew radio ahead to St. Joe's emergency room, ensuring that an operating room would be ready with a neonatal specialist and obstetrical team standing by.

"Boy, this little girl really wants to make a dramatic entrance, huh?" Morgan was worried sick about the baby, but she did her best to reassure Pam and Frank with as much light chatter as she could manage. "Don't get too upset, either of you. She's got a great chance of coming though this fine,'' she lied as perspiration dripped from her chin and her arm trembled as if she had palsy.

In moments they screamed into St. Joe's emergency bay, and in spite of her acute discomfort, Morgan felt a proprietary pride in the swift, efficient way Pam was transferred from ambulance to operating room, with Morgan perched on the end of the stretcher, still steadfastly pushing the baby into the pelvis. She'd jettisoned her high heels back at the church, and she was gasping with the strain. She was on the verge of collapse.

Another two minutes. You can do it, Jacobsen....

''Here we are. The gang's all here and everything's gonna be just fine. Good girl, Pam. Are you ever brave...'' she said as the charge nurse whisked Frank to an adjoining room.

Pam's clothing was swiftly removed, and both Pam and Morgan were covered and draped. Then the anesthetist began the exacting procedure of administering general anesthesia. Morgan had just enough stamina left to be pleased that Jeffrey Liung, who'd taken over her previous position as chief resident in obstetrics, was the doctor who'd be doing the Caesarean. Jeffrey was top-notch—she knew because she'd trained him.

At last, Pam was under.

"Ohh, hurry up, Doc. My arm's going to fall off," Morgan groaned to Jeffrey. He was already quickly cutting through the abdominal layers with his scalpel.

"How's baby doing?" Morgan couldn't see the monitor.

"Heart rate's flat," a nurse said softly.

Morgan could sense the tension in the room, and her heart sank. There was none of the usual cheerful chatter or bantering. The only sounds were the hissing of the machines and the clatter of used instruments as they clanged into a pan.

She gritted her teeth and endured, refusing to think about disaster.

Jeffrey was now in the uterus, stretching the incision carefully but firmly. An intern pushed down on the top of the uterus to give leverage as Jeffrey slid one hand into the incision.

"Gotcha, little one." There was both relief and alarm in everyone's eyes as he lifted the baby's head and turned it to keep the infant from sucking in any fluid. The head came out slowly, a tiny round ball topped with wet black hair.

Morgan groaned, at last able to remove her aching, trembling arm from Pam's pelvis and straighten from her contorted position.

The doctors immediately inserted a bulb syringe in the baby's mouth, suctioning mucous as Jeffrey eased the rest of the tiny body out of Pam's womb. The baby girl was small but perfectly formed—and dark blue. The neonatal specialist whisked her to a separate area the moment the cord was severed.

Morgan stepped shakily down from the table. No matter how many times she witnessed birth, she usually felt an overwhelming surge of tenderness and acute wonder at this first emergence of a human being into the world. This time, however, there was gut-wrenching apprehension because she was well aware that this scrap of a girl might not make it. Her birth had been traumatic in the extreme.

Morgan glanced over at the table where the specialist was working over the limp and still baby, and she uttered a silent, passionate prayer to the angels that she believed hovered over every mother and child at this moment of birth. *Thank you for saving this precious child,* she repeated to herself. She tried to feel only expectant confidence, but her heart hammered with apprehension as precious seconds ticked away.

Streaks of blood were shockingly bright against the white, sticky vernix that covered the baby's skin, and the awful tension in the room intensified as the silence stretched unbearably.

And then, to everyone's delight, the baby suddenly startled and gave a choked, squawking cry.

A ragged cheer went up from the entire team.

"That's my sweetheart," Morgan crowed as more short, sharp cries came from the baby. Her skin pinkened and her tiny limbs thrashed.

"Sounding good, young lady," the specialist declared in a pleased tone. "Apgar's six, so it'll be a while before we know for sure, but my guess is she's going to be fine," he told Morgan a few moments later after examining the baby thoroughly.

Morgan nodded, too choked up to even answer. Tears spilled out of her eyes, and she felt like whooping with joy or singing at the top of her lungs. She compromised by doing a spirited little tap dance, and everyone laughed, all of them used to her antics.

"I'm going to give Frank the good news, and then maybe I ought to go and get cleaned up a little." Morgan flexed her aching shoulders and sent a fervent thank-you to the angels as the team applied themselves to the laborious task of cleaning and repairing Pam's abdominal cavity.

The nurses who were assisting knew both Pam and Celia, and now that the emergency was over they plied Morgan with questions about the wedding ceremony, shaking their heads in amazement and then laughing when she told them about the wine.

"The pastor thought it was for me, and boy, was I tempted," she joked. "One thing for sure—nobody who was there today is ever likely to forget Celia's wedding."

They all laughed again, and Morgan lingered a moment longer, enjoying the warm, cozy sense of family she experienced so often here in the delivery room after the safe arrival of a child.

Here she knew exactly who she was and what she'd been born to do.

CHAPTER TWO

MORGAN WENT STRAIGHT from the emergency OR to talk to Frank, giving him a congratulatory hug and then taking all the time necessary to explain exactly what had occurred. It was the better part of an hour before Pam's abdomen was repaired, and the moment the procedure was over, Morgan took Frank to Pam's bedside in recovery.

She was there when her patient awakened, able to witness Pam holding her daughter for the first time, and Morgan's heart overflowed with joy when she finally left the little family alone.

In the bathroom, she sang at the top of her lungs as she scrubbed her face and hands, aware for the first time that her dress was a spectacular mess, bloodstained, creased and even torn near the hem. She mopped halfheartedly at the worst of the stains with a dripping cloth, remembering too late that the blue fabric puckered when it got wet.

Drat. Now the skirt rucked up in front so that her slip showed in a wide white arc.

Well, she was properly wrecked, but what the heck. It was for a good cause. Besides, she'd snatched the dress off a sale rack two days before because she had nothing suitable for the wedding, not because it had been an inspired choice.

Not that she *ever* had inspired choices where clothing was concerned, she told herself with a wry grin at the mirror, noting that the freckles on her nose were standing out like signposts and her red curls looked as if an electric current had recently passed through them.

Rain always did that to her hair. She needed a hairbrush in the worst way, and she remembered now that she'd left her purse on the seat of the pew in the church. Her keys were in it, as well as her wallet, which meant she was going to have to borrow cab fare to get back to the church and rescue her belongings.

It suddenly dawned on her that her shoes were also missing. She looked down at her bare toes protruding from what was left of her panty hose, and she had to giggle at this final calamity. She hiked up her skirt and stripped the hose off, tossing them into the wastebasket before heading for the staff lounge. With any luck there'd be someone around with ten dollars they could lend her for taxi fare. She burst into the lounge whistling a cheerful tune, and stopped short.

"Dr. Jacobsen? Good heavens, what's happened to you?"

The cultured voice with its distinctive English accent belonged to a tall, broad-shouldered man in an impeccably tailored gray suit over a soft white shirt and charcoal silk tie.

Like her, Luke Gilbert was an obstetrician. Unlike her, he dressed for success. When Morgan first met him, she couldn't believe anyone would wear such obviously expensive clothes to deliver babies.

Lean and graceful, he was seated now on the old brown couch under the high window, one ankle propped on the opposite knee. The overhead light glanced across the clean, strong bones of his face as he stared at her. After a second he rose to his feet and walked closer, towering over her, his thick dark brows furrowed as he took in the full extent of the damage.

"You've had an accident?" He had a good mouth, but he didn't use it for smiling much.

Morgan resisted the urge to tug her puckered dress down over her bare knees. "Nope, just an emergency delivery. It was really something—cord prolapse." She explained the circumstances, doing her best to mask the intense discomfort and annoyance she felt. "We had a beautiful baby girl. Kind of flat at first but a real winner when she got going. All's well that ends well.''

Morgan hoped she sounded a lot more breezy than she felt. Wouldn't you know that flawless Dr. Gilbert would be around just when she was looking her absolute worst? Of all the doctors she knew, he was the last one she'd have chosen to see today. Any day, actually. He bothered her in a way she couldn't rationally explain.

''I've had only one prolapse myself. It's not my idea of a good time,'' he remarked.

''Mine, either. Especially not in church.''

Four years ago, there'd been intense excitement and high speculation among the female staff at St. Joe's when this man appeared on the scene. Morgan had been working at the hospital then as chief resident in obstetrics. She remembered how the hospital grapevine quickly circulated the fact that Dr. Gilbert was thirty-six, a recent widower and the father of an eleven-year-old daughter.

Gossip had it he'd moved to Vancouver from Victoria when his wife died in a car accident. He'd joined a small general practice, but his specialty was OB-GYN.

It was obvious to every woman who ever laid eyes on him that he was all male and totally desirable, and Morgan hadn't been impervious to his attraction, although she didn't like to admit it to herself. She'd certainly never told a living soul that he'd starred in a series of highly erotic dreams that plagued her for months. She was long over them now, thank goodness, but the memory still made her highly uncomfortable around him.

During his first few months at St. Joe's, Morgan had watched as he was actively pursued by a stampede of eager females, but the furor had eventually died down. Word went out that Luke Gilbert was polite, remote—and unavailable. It soon became evident that he spent most of his time working; he even volunteered several evenings a week in the ER. Anyone who did that was tagged a hopeless workaholic.

Morgan knew him professionally, of course. They'd even consulted occasionally. He had a good reputation, and she'd seen him often before she'd taken the job at Women's Place.

She hadn't seen him much since leaving the hospital, and she hadn't missed him, either, Morgan assured herself. Luke Gilbert was too well-groomed, too quiet, too self-contained, too unemotional. All the things she emphatically wasn't. How could a man who'd chosen to deliver babies be unemotional, for Pete's sake?

"Can I be of any assistance, Morgan? You seem to have lost your shoes." She realized he was trying not to stare at her bare feet, and she suddenly found it funny that he'd be the one in the lounge at this precise moment. She grinned up at him, way up.... He was more than a foot taller than her.

"The shoes don't matter, but I need to borrow some money, Luke. Ten dollars if you can spare it, for a taxi. I left my purse at the church, and my Jeep's in a lot on Davie Street."

"Of course." He was pulling out a leather wallet before she finished speaking, holding out a twenty. "I'd take you down to get your Jeep myself," he said as he proffered the money, "but I've got a patient arriving who sounds as if she's about to deliver."

"No problem. I can call a cab. Thanks a lot." Morgan accepted the bill, careful not to touch his fingers. She was uncomfortably aware of his nearness, and also of the fact that she hadn't gotten all the blood specks off her arm.

"I'll get this back to you. I'll leave the money with Edna next time I'm in." Edna was everyone's favorite nurse on Maternity.

"Perhaps we could arrange to meet for lunch one day next week instead?" Luke's green eyes met hers, and one brow lifted in inquiry.

For an insane moment, Morgan misunderstood, and something inside her went still.

"You see, I'd very much like to talk to you about Women's Place," he added. "I've taken a position there. Jenkins had me in for an interview a week ago last Friday, and it went well. As you probably know, I've been doing general practice, but I'd prefer to get back to my specialty. It seems we'll be working together.''

Morgan could only stare at him, dumbfounded.

Luke Gilbert, working with her at Women's Place? Of course she'd known the small, popular clinic had to hire another doctor. She was the one who'd insisted that there was far too much work for the staff they had, that they were forced to turn too many patients away.

An uncharacteristic torrent of confused and angry emotion swept over her. Too much work or not, the one thing she was absolutely certain of, even though she didn't fully understand why, was that she did not—*did not*—want Luke Gilbert working with her.

She wouldn't have him, and that was that. She'd tell Jenkins first thing Monday morning that Dr. Gilbert was the only obstetrician in the entire western hemisphere with whom she simply could not get along.

She remembered now that Jenkins had called her several times this past week, asking her to return his messages, and of course she hadn't. She'd been run off her feet. With a sinking feeling in her stomach, she remembered also that she'd turned down his offer to interview suitable applicants. Again, she'd simply been too busy.

Well, she'd have to make her position clear now, despite her earlier carelessness. Incompatible personalities, she'd claim. Or should that be conflicting beliefs? Whatever the wording, the meaning was the same.

"About lunch," she managed to croak. "I'll have to check my appointment book and let you know." As if she'd ever kept such a thing as an up-to-date personal appointment book.

"Of course. Whenever it's convenient," he agreed in that terribly polite English fashion.

That'll be about two weeks after hell freezes over. "Good. I'll be in touch then," she said with a bright, phony smile and a silly wave as she headed out the door and down the hall.

She phoned for a cab and was standing on the sidewalk in front of the Emergency exit waiting for its arrival before she realized it was raining harder than ever and her feet were still bare.

SHE WAS THE MOST peculiar little woman. Luke knew she was one of the most sought-after obstetricians in the city, and she was certainly the only woman he'd ever met who paid no attention whatsoever to her appearance.

He shook his head. He'd actually thought for an instant that she'd been assaulted, with her dress stained and askew, her shapely legs and tiny feet bare of shoes or stockings. She looked far more like a wayward child than a doctor if you discounted the ample breasts underneath that hideous garment she'd been wearing.

Luke stood where she'd left him, wondering what he'd said to cause the hostility so evident in her eyes and voice before she'd scampered away. She had the translucent skin that so often went with that shade of fiery hair, and he suspected she had a temper to match. Bright flags of angry color had stained her high cheekbones, and her big chocolate brown eyes had flashed a warning at him, as if he'd insulted her instead of simply suggesting a business lunch.

Women. He didn't begin to understand them, in spite of the fact that his work necessitated contact of the most intimate sort. With a hiss of impatience, he dismissed Morgan Jacobsen and stalked off to find out what had become of his patient.

FORTY-FIVE MINUTES after she'd left St. Joe's, Morgan finally drove her battered red Jeep into the garage behind her house, grateful to be home at last. She climbed out, wincing as the dratted beige pumps rubbed at the blister on her right heel. So much for shoving bare wet feet into uncomfortable shoes, she thought as she climbed the rickety back stairs. *Must see about getting these steps replaced this week.*

The old house she'd bought constantly needed something fixed, and she thought that was probably why it had appealed to her so much. Perfection just wasn't her thing.

She opened the door, and a blast of rock music greeted her. Nirvana.

Obviously her foster daughter, Tessa, was home, and there'd been no sign of Dylan Volger's motorcycle in the driveway, which was a relief. Morgan was not fond of Tessa's boyfriend.

"Hi, Tess," she hollered, bracing herself against the ecstatic barrage of animals that met her just inside the kitchen door. "Major, sit." The floppy-eared golden retriever dropped obediently to the floor, but Skippy, the small black poodle, went on jumping and barking a shrill, high greeting. He was deaf, and Morgan was trying to teach him some signs, but it wasn't working very well. He bounded around hysterically while Flower, the kitten, wound intricate patterns around her ankles.

"I'm in here," Tessa yelled above the racket, and Morgan limped across the kitchen and into the living room.

"Hiya, Morgan. So, how was the wedding?" Tessa Hargraves uncurled herself from the depths of the old green couch in front of the fireplace and struggled to her feet. She still had ten weeks before her due date, and even though her baby was small, her skinny fifteen-year-old frame still seemed too fragile to bear the weight of her pregnancy.

She looked at Morgan and whistled between her teeth. "Man, look at you. You're a disaster. And you're soaked to the skin! What the heck happened to that dress?" She tipped her head with its purple spikes of hair to one side and regarded Morgan curiously.

"I'll never wear these blasted shoes again." Morgan kicked them off and bent down to stroke and pat her menagerie, raising her voice to be heard. "Turn the stereo down a couple of hundred decibels, would you, please?"

Tessa went over to the wall unit, and the music subsided to a bearable level. "Want some tea? I made chocolate chip cookies—they turned out pretty good." Her heart-shaped face shone with pride at her accomplishment. She'd never cooked before she'd come to live at Morgan's four months ago, but it was fast becoming her hobby.

"I'd love some. Put the kettle on and I'll go upstairs and change. Can you believe this dress?"

Tessa studied the hopelessly puckered garment, and a gamin grin spread across her pretty features. "Looks like you oughta take it back and tell 'em it shrank when you took a bath in it." She giggled, and when Morgan did a clumsy pirouette, they both laughed aloud.

Ten minutes later, in comfortable, worn jeans and a much-washed sweatshirt that might have once been green, Morgan walked, still barefoot, into the kitchen. Tessa had cleared a small space amidst the clutter on the antique wooden table. Two mismatched mugs sat waiting beside an enormous yellow teapot and a platter of lumpy cookies.

Morgan plopped down on a chair with a grateful sigh. The dogs vied for the most strategic position and finally arranged themselves at her feet, while Flower, the small marmalade kitten with only one eye, settled on her lap. Flower was Morgan's most recent acquisition from the pound.

"Okay, so what went down? Like, how'd you get totally destroyed just going to a wedding?" Tessa bit half a cookie and munched on it, her wide hazel eyes filled with anticipation as Morgan began to talk, deliberately leaving out the serious aspects of Pam's situation and turning the dramatic events of the day into a comedy for her foster daughter's enjoyment.

"And would you believe the organist went

right on playing right through the whole thing...."

Outside, the rainy Saturday afternoon darkened into evening. Water spilled down the windowpanes and gurgled in the gutters, and as she talked, Morgan was aware of the cosiness of her kitchen, of the contentment and happiness that filled her. She relished the growing closeness she and Tessa seemed to be developing. It had been hard at first to gain even a fraction of the girl's trust.

The fact that Morgan disliked and distrusted Dylan Vogler, the seventeen-year-old youth who'd fathered Tessa's baby, had caused heated discussions between them and a certain amount of resentment on Tessa's part.

But the young girl looked relaxed and even happy today, Morgan mused as she described in hilarious detail looking into the mirror after the emergency was over, finding blood all over her face, realizing her feet were bare and her slip showing. Tessa's chortling giggle delighted her.

Four short months ago, when Tessa had first come to live with her, Morgan had wondered if the youngster had ever smiled in her entire life, or had a decent meal, either. But Tessa had put on a few much needed pounds recently. Her face was slightly fuller than it had been, her arms a shade less skeletal. And Morgan was less concerned about the baby than she'd been at first. Good nutrition and the fact that Tess had stopped smoking had greatly improved the chances that the fetus would reach normal birth weight.

Morgan felt like thumbing her nose at the people who'd felt compelled to make dire predictions of doom when she'd first decided to take Tessa Hargraves into her home.

Tessa had been in foster care most of her short life, she had a gold ring in her right nostril, another in her left eyebrow and six more in each ear. She was tough, streetwise, rebellious and pregnant, which even Morgan had to admit was a daunting combination, but the experiment was working out well.

It would be even better if Tessa dumped Dylan, but perhaps that was too much to ask, too soon.

All in all, it was great fun having a foster daughter, Morgan mused. It was wonderful to have someone to come home to on a rainy afternoon. Much as she adored her dogs and the kitten, they'd sure never managed to make her tea and cookies.

So the kitchen was a bit of a disaster area, with pots and mixing bowls scattered on every surface, and drying remnants of chocolate dough spattered on the floor, the counter and the cupboard doors. This mess didn't bother Morgan one bit. Messes never had. To her, people mattered. Animals mattered. Feelings mattered. Messes? Phooey. They could always be mopped up.

A mental image of Luke Gilbert popped into her head. Messes would definitely drive him nuts. She wondered what sort of things really mattered to a man like him.

Propriety. Tidiness. Decorum. Doing and saying the right thing, she thought scornfully. Well, phooey to Luke Gilbert.

"These cookies are super," she pronounced with a shade more enthusiasm than was called for. They were slightly charred on the outside and underdone in the middle, but Morgan chewed with honest appreciation.

She'd find time soon to teach Tessa all the finer details of baking and cooking, she promised herself. Cooking was definitely an interest she and Tessa shared, one they could work at together.

Working together. The words brought once again a clear-cut image of Luke's strong jaw with its distinctive cleft, his perfectly cut black hair, his immaculate suit, and once again panic threatened.

She could and would make her feelings

known to Jenkins first thing Monday morning.

*Please, God, let Luke Gilbert find a better job
far, far away from me and decide to take it.*

CHAPTER THREE

MORGAN WAS CALLED OUT at 3:00 a.m. that Sunday morning to deliver a baby girl. A gorgeous baby girl, she rejoiced as she crawled back into bed just before seven, weary to the bone.

Her throat felt raw and scratchy. Too tired to get up and search for lozenges, she slid into a restless sleep, waking at eleven forty-five to the muted beat of the stereo downstairs. Her throat had gone from scratchy to inflamed, and her entire body ached. She was also shivering, which meant she probably had a fever.

Morgan's reaction to any illness that dared threaten her busy life had always been to ignore the symptoms until they went away, insulted by her lack of attention. All her years of training had taught her to put her own needs last. Determined to do so now, she forced herself out of bed and into a hot shower. She did feel much better when she finally made it downstairs, but a scant hour later, the vomiting began.

"I bet you've got that killer flu going around," Tessa said, watching Morgan stagger out of the downstairs bathroom for the fourth time, shivering as if the gas fireplace weren't going full blast. "You better get up to bed. I'll make you some mint tea."

"I'll be fine by morning," Morgan insisted through gritted teeth, clinging to the banister. "I'll be over this by morning—I have to be. I need to get to the clinic. And you stay away from me. I'm contagious and you sure don't need to catch this. Think of Kyla Jean."

Tessa had named her baby the moment she learned through ultrasound that it was a girl.

For Morgan, the night passed in a torment of fevered dreams and urgent trips to the bathroom. Tessa came in once, bleary-eyed and concerned, and Morgan lied and assured her she was getting much better.

A firm believer in letting nature take its course, she finally gave in at dawn and took some medication, but it didn't seem to have much effect.

Tessa arrived at seven with a cookie sheet laden with a mug of tea and a slice of plain toast, but the very smell of food made Morgan's stomach twist in rebellion.

"Maybe you'd better call Rachel and say I can't make it in this morning. Tell her to cancel my appointments," Morgan moaned. "Tell her I'll be there this afternoon for sure."

"Maybe I'd better say it's gonna be a day or two, huh?" Tessa's forehead creased with concern. "You don't look so hot. Shouldn't you be taking something?"

"Did. Didn't work."

"So what can I do?" Tessa handed Morgan a cold washcloth for her head.

"Nothing. Get out of here. Go to school before you catch it." She knew she sounded cranky; she totally despised being sick, but she shouldn't snap at Tessa. She made a monumental effort at a smile and failed miserably. "Sorry for being a grump. Go now. I'll be fine by tonight. This is just a twenty-four-hour thing. It'll pass."

But the fever climbed as the day progressed, and that evening she developed a racking cough. By Tuesday morning she was so drained she could hardly get out of bed.

"You need a doctor," Tessa declared, scowling down at her. She changed the sheets and helped Morgan into a dry nightshirt. The tea and toast she'd brought again sat untouched on the tray. "You haven't eaten a thing since Sunday, and now your eyes are all black underneath. Don't you figure maybe I oughta call a doctor?"

"I *am* a doctor," Morgan reminded her, but her voice quavered with weakness. "And I'm pretty sure this thing has run its course. I'll start feeling better today, you watch and see. Lots of liquids, that's the ticket.''

Tessa looked doubtful, but she didn't say anything. She brought up a fresh jug of water and some orange juice, and Morgan fell in and out of sleep all morning. She was pitifully grateful when Tessa came home shortly past noon.

"I told Mrs. Nelson I was taking the afternoon off because you were sick. I'll need a note tomorrow."

"Sure." Would she even be able to write by then?

"Maybe help me into the shower, Tess. I think a hot shower might do me good." She was shivering again, and she was shocked at her own weakness and impressed at how her ribs and pelvic bones stuck out when she stripped her nightshirt off. Losing a few pounds wasn't a bad thing, but as soon as Tessa was out of the room, Morgan leaned close to the mirror and pulled up her eyelid. She stared at her eyeball. Was it yellow? She wasn't sure. She pinched the skin on her forearm. Maybe it looked sort of yellowish. Had she been exposed to something toxic in the lab?

Or maybe she'd caught hepatitis B. She shuddered. She'd been immunized, but that was a long time ago. What if it hadn't taken the way it was supposed to?

In the shower, she could barely stay upright under the hot spray, and waves of dizziness undulated over her. She didn't even have enough energy to brush her hair when she got out. She simply toweled herself off with Tessa's help, dragged on a gown and slunk back into bed. It was a huge relief to be lying down again.

"You still figure this is just a dose of the flu?" There was palpable worry in Tessa's tone.

"'Course." Morgan wasn't at all sure. Her brain teemed with nightmarish symptoms that might be developing.

"I'll have a little nap and then maybe we could have some soup or something," she said, even though the very thought of food made her gag. She could feel the fever beginning to build again, and she curled into a miserable ball under the mound of covers, her body racked by shudders.

"Maybe you could fill the hot-water bottle for me again, hon? Cold in here."

Tessa gave her a long, troubled look and then headed for the bathroom, and Morgan slid back into the disjointed state that passed for sleep.

LUKE HAD JUST delivered twins, a boy and a girl, by caesarean section, to Anna Zenobin, a thirty-six-year-old patient of Morgan Jacobsen's. He should have felt elated because the procedure had gone relatively well, but all he could think of was the consultation with Anna before the operation, which had been nothing short of disaster.

It was clear from the first moment that Anna considered him an inadequate substitute for Morgan. The fact was, Anna had burst into stormy tears when Luke arrived in her labor room and explained quietly that Dr. Jacobsen was ill and that he was taking her calls. And when he mentioned a caesarean, Anna had become hysterical.

"I want Morgan," she'd wailed. "We planned every single part of how this would go. She promised me she'd be here with me. She promised we'd try a vaginal delivery. I need her! I need her!"

It had taken enormous patience and a great deal of time to calm her down. It took more quiet reassurance to convince her that because the membranes had ruptured, and that, in his opinion, a caesarean was now necessary, any other option would seriously compromise her babies.

Of course Luke suppressed the annoyance he felt at being treated like a second-class bungler. Damn Morgan Jacobsen, anyhow. What was it about that little woman that aroused such fanatic loyalty in her patients? He knew himself to be every bit as competent an obstetrician, but in two short days of dealing with Morgan's patients, he'd come to realize that each and every one of them regarded her as some ridiculous combination of miracle worker, saint and, most preposterous of all, intimate friend.

What was she thinking of, encouraging patients to relate on such personal terms? To him, it violated every tenet of doctor-patient ethics. And to top it all off, he got a call from the clinic just as he was leaving the hospital saying that Morgan's daughter had phoned and asked if someone would make a house call because Morgan wasn't getting better. And being the only doctor working late, he was nominated.

Bloody hell.

Luke darted between lanes, recklessly squeezing his sporty little black car into nonexistent gaps in the stream of vehicles around him. It took all his concentration, which was the whole point.

He didn't want to have to think.

The address was in an old residential neighborhood near the university. The Tudor-style house was big and weathered by time, the exterior covered in stained honey-colored stucco with vines growing up both stories. The property was bordered by low juniper bushes behind a wire fence. It was an attractive home, he admitted grudgingly as he opened the gate and made his way up the front path, trudging through ankle-deep autumn leaves.

The front door could have used a new coat of paint, though, he noticed as he rang the doorbell. Dogs barked inside, and it was several moments before the door opened.

A fist seemed to smash into Luke's gut when he saw the girl standing in the doorway. She looked about the same age as his daughter.

"Oh, hi. You must be Doc Gilbert, right? I'm Tessa Hargraves—Morgan's foster kid? I'm really glad you're here. Morgan's, like, *really* sick." She scowled at the dogs, still yapping. "Major, shush. Skippy, can it, would ya? C'mon in, Doc. She's upstairs in bed and she's gonna blow a gasket when she finds out I called you, but I'm really worried about her, y'know?"

This girl had none of Sophie's soft, plump blond beauty. This girl's arms and legs were long and thin. She was taller, too, her spiky hair cut short and dyed fluorescent purple. Her face was a perfect heart shape, marred by a gold ring in one nostril, another in an eyebrow and what looked like dozens up the lobes of her ears. Sophie wore only small pearls, one in each ear.

Tessa's eyes were heavily made-up. Of course he didn't allow Sophie, at only fifteen, to use makeup in that tawdry way.

This girl wore a garish oversize yellow T-shirt over black tights, and her protruding belly made Luke's stomach heave and clench as he automatically stepped over the threshold and into the midst of the dogs, who sniffed at his pant legs and wagged their tails. The black poodle was still yapping at him.

"Skippy's deaf and neurotic. You can't shut him up once he gets goin'," Tessa explained. "C'mon, Doc Gilbert, she's up here."

Tessa's back was narrow and childlike as she climbed the stairs ahead of him, but the weight of her belly made her waddle a bit. Sophie would walk like that before long, losing her quickness and grace as her pregnancy developed.

His little girl, his baby, his only child, was pregnant, too. The knowledge made the hard knot that now seemed a permanent fixture in his chest tighten and burn as if acid were being dripped on his heart.

What in God's name was he going to do about it?

What in God's name could he do?

"Morgan?" The deep voice with its distinctive accent was at first part of her confused dream. "Morgan, wake up."

She opened heavy eyelids and decided she was delirious.

Luke Gilbert stood beside the bed, wearing gray slacks, navy blazer and an elegant tie against a gleaming white-on-white striped shirt. He'd placed his medical bag on the chair beside the bed, the same chair where her lacy bra and pink flowered bikini panties lay from the last time she'd dressed. She remembered groggily that her housecoat, jeans, several sweaters and a few pairs of socks were in an untidy heap on the floor.

"What are *you* doing *here?*" Her voice sounded like a foghorn, and she knew she looked as bad as she ever had in her entire life.

She saw him glance at the kitten, Flower, who had her head tucked under the spare pillow. Morgan noticed for the first time that there were cat hairs on the blue sheets.

"He's here because of me," Tessa said in a defensive tone. "I called the clinic and asked for a doctor to come and look at you. I'm scared you're gettin' worse."

"I'd have been here earlier, but I was doing a section. Mrs. Zenobin's twins arrived a bit early. I've just come from the hospital," he said in an offhand tone.

"Anna's twins? You sectioned Anna's twins?" Morgan struggled to a sitting position, feeling as if she might burst into tears. The twins' arrival had been an event she'd looked forward to for months. She and Anna Zenobin had talked about every aspect of the babies' delivery, and now she'd missed it. And he'd done a C-section, probably unnecessarily. Anna would never forgive her. She'd never forgive herself.

"A boy and a girl, both good babies. The membranes had ruptured, and there was distress on the monitor. There was a bit of excitement with the girl—she'd aspirated meconium and was a bit flat by the time we got her out. She's in ICU. I checked just before coming over, and she's doing well. We've got her on an antibiotic drip."

"You felt it was absolutely necessary to do a section?" Morgan had discussed the method of birth with Anna at length, explaining that most multiple births were sectioned, but promising Anna that if the babies were large enough and Anna had no complications, Morgan would be willing to try for a vaginal delivery.

"Of course I sectioned her. It was a premature multiple birth, and that was the only option, in my opinion."

"I disagree," Morgan said with all the vehemence she could muster. "Anna's not a primipara. Her other pregnancy and delivery were entirely normal, and I'd promised her we'd give vaginal delivery a try if everything looked good."

"I gathered that's what you'd told her. Needless to say, it caused some unnecessary upset for both me and the mother when I explained my policy on multiple births."

He bent over his bag to retrieve a thermometer, and Morgan felt like booting him for what she considered his pigheaded attitude.

She felt too sick to get into an argument with him just now, but she was angry all the same. She scowled at Tessa, standing at the foot of the bed, irked with her for calling him.

Tessa's T-shirt had tomato paste smeared down the front, and she looked messy, guilty and worried. Her baby moved beneath the cotton, and Morgan's anger disappeared as quickly as it had come. After all, it wasn't anyone's fault but her own that she was sick, and Tessa was doing the best she knew how.

"It's okay, love. I'm not going to die," Morgan croaked, scowling at Luke as he took her temperature. He palpated the glands in her throat and looked into her ears, pushing aside her thick, tangled hair with cool, impersonal fingers.

She thought of mentioning hepatitis B and decided he could damn well diagnose it without her help.

He used his stethoscope to listen to her lungs, and she was excruciatingly aware that only a thin layer of cotton lay between her breasts and his long, elegant fingers. Even his nails were perfect, she noted sourly, square and smooth and immaculate. Morgan curled her own chipped and broken nails into fists and stuck them beneath the covers, wondering if she had the acidic, sick smell people got when they ran high fevers.

During his examination he bent close, and unless she closed her eyes, she couldn't help but look at him. His face was dramatic—quite spectacularly handsome, except that it resembled a carved stone mask and betrayed not one single human emotion. Even his green eyes were as cool and remote as a mountain pond.

Morgan tried not to cough on him and wondered why someone so devoid of feeling would have settled on obstetrics as a career. Pathology seemed a much more likely match for Dr. Gilbert.

"Your temperature is elevated and the glands in your neck are enlarged," he pronounced in a distant tone. She'd heard total strangers sound more animated while discussing the weather. "There's a virulent strain of influenza going round. I suspect that's what you've got, Doctor, but I'd like to take some throat swabs and do a blood workup just to be certain."

He swabbed and she gagged and gave him a filthy look. She had to admit he was slick with a needle, though; he fixed a tourniquet just above her elbow, and she barely felt the prick as he drew a vial of blood.

"Aaagh, gross." Tessa winced in sympathy as the dark blood welled into the vial. She moved to the opposite side of the bed and gripped Morgan's other hand with both of her own, her face pale.

"It doesn't hurt, sweetie." Morgan gave her a weak smile.

"So, like, what can I do to help her get better, Doc Gilbert?" The girl's voice quavered a little, and she frowned up at him. "Like, shouldn't she be eating something? I'm making this special vegetable soup. D'ya think soup'll help?"

Tessa's plaintive appeal almost brought tears to Morgan's eyes, but it was all too obvious that Luke was untouched by the young girl's plea. "Bed rest and liquids," he pronounced in a dismissive tone, turning away. He didn't so much as glance at Tessa as he packed his things in meticulous order back into his bag.

"So what'ya think, Luke? Is there a faint chance I'm going to live?" Morgan tried her best to lighten the atmosphere for Tessa's sake.

"As I said, rest and plenty of fluids. I'll leave something to control the fever and vomiting." Luke spoke without looking at her. He seemed to be staring at the thick layer of dust on the cluttered dresser, and his clipped tone held not one iota of personal concern or warmth. He hadn't smiled once or been the slightest bit friendly, and rage suddenly consumed her. It was probably the fever that made her reckless.

"Darn you, Luke Gilbert! Who exactly do you think you are, acting so condescending and superior?" Her voice, contralto at the best of times, had dropped to a croaky bass, but fortunately nothing had affected her volume control, and his head whipped around. At least he was looking at her now.

Good, so she had his full attention. "Haven't you ever gotten sick, or are people as perfect as you immune to everything?" She realized she was borderline hysterical, but she didn't care one whit. "Haven't you...haven't you ever thrown your underwear on a chair? Isn't there ever dust on your dresser?" This tirade was taking enormous energy, and she could feel herself trembling and getting dizzy. "You've got a daughter. Can't you see how worried Tessa is, how she needs your reassurance?"

She paused for breath, panting and weak. "So help me, most first-year interns have a better bedside manner than you have, Luke Gilbert. Can't you come down off your high horse and get human for once in your life?"

Luke stared at Morgan, and the only indication that her words had had any effect was a tightening of his jaw and a quick flash of emotion that came and went in his eyes.

He was silent. He set several vials on the bedside table, and with unshakable dignity, picked up his bag and moved toward the door.

Tessa was frozen in place beside the bed. Morgan realized that the girl had never seen her lose her temper to that extent. Morgan sank back on her pillows, shuddering as if her body were about to break apart.

"Oh, phooey." Tears formed in her eyes and rolled slowly down her cheeks. She'd said what she felt, all right, but she had a horrible niggling feeling that Luke had come out the victor, just by maintaining his cool.

CHAPTER FOUR

LUKE MADE HIS WAY down the stairwell, his mind registering the worn but colorful carpet, the stained-glass window on the landing, the lovely old desk that stood beside the front door. A shiny tin can held a casual bouquet of dying roses, pink and gold petals mounded in a soft heap at its base.

Major came limping from the recesses of the house, tail wagging and tongue lolling. Luke automatically bent to rub a hand over his silky head, noting that there was something wrong with the dog's hind legs. He limped noticeably.

"Stay, fellow," he ordered in a soft tone, and Major obediently dropped to his belly on the floor as Luke let himself out and closed the door quietly behind him.

His heart was hammering and his throat felt dry. He ran a finger around his collar. It was choking him. He climbed into his car and started it. He sped away from the curb, squealed around a corner and made his way down the long hill to Southwest Marine Drive.

He punched a button and the radio blared to life, but even the frantic patter of a local deejay couldn't muffle the echo of Morgan's voice.

You've got a daughter...a daughter...a daughter.... Can't you see how she needs your reassurance...reassurance...reassurance...

He drove with automatic expertise, but the road and traffic were superseded in his mind by the image of a wild, red-haired woman, curls standing up like Medusa's snakes, freckles on her straight nose in bas relief against the extreme pallor of her silken skin. And her eyes. Those huge, expressive chocolate brown eyes were filled with contempt as she verbalized all the wretched things he knew to be true about himself.

She was right about him. There wasn't dust on his dresser; he did hang his clothing up the moment he removed it; he'd always paid meticulous attention to his grooming. Part of that was due to the years he'd spent in an English public school, but he supposed a shrink would say he imposed rigid control over his environment because it was so absolutely *out* of control.

She'd said his bedside manner was atrocious. He knew he didn't project warmth or friendliness the way Morgan did. He couldn't possibly allow his emotions free rein, permitting whatever he was feeling to show on his face or in his voice, because a single crack in the iron facade he'd so carefully erected would bring the entire structure down in ruins.

One simply couldn't commit murder. Men didn't cry. And he couldn't reassure his daughter, or Morgan's, either, because he didn't know what words to use. He'd decided long ago that he was illiterate when it came to love, and certainly the events of his life had proven that to be true.

That girl, Tessa. He saw her as if her picture were glued to the windshield, her protruding belly like a small, hard balloon attached to her skinny frame, holding Morgan's hand in both her own, her wide eyes mirroring concern behind their mascaraed lashes.

Damnation. He smashed his fist down on the steering wheel. Sophie's stubborn, impassive face was also as clear as a photograph in his mind's eye, her wide-set gray eyes avoiding any contact with his, her rosy mouth downturned, her body held stiff and tight should he reach out and put a hand on her shoulder or arm. Lately, each time he'd tried, she'd jerked herself away.

At last he was home. He wheeled into his circular driveway. The gardener had raked the leaves and taken them away. The house was pristine and perfect. Luke had bought it new, directly from the contractor who'd built it, Adam

Hendricks, and Adam and Luke had become friends as they worked out the details of the purchase. Adam and his pretty wife, Peggy, had welcomed Luke and his daughter into the bosom of their large, noisy family.

And then Adam's son, Jason, had made Sophie pregnant.

He inserted his key in the door.

"Evening, Dr. Gilbert." His housekeeper was waiting in the hall, and he remembered now that she'd wanted to have dinner early tonight.

"Hello, Eileen. Sorry I'm late, I had a house call to make, but I should have phoned. My apologies." Luke removed his shoes and set them side by side in the hall closet, sliding his feet into the moccasins he kept there. Eileen was fussy about the floors.

He glanced around at the gleaming surfaces of his home, the carefully polished silver tea service on the low coffee table, the carpets without a trace of lint, the careful arrangements of silk flowers set here and there. Eileen was a terrific housekeeper, no doubt about it. He'd had several housekeepers after Deborah died, none of them good. He'd hired Eileen when he moved from Victoria, and she'd lasted.

It was unfortunate that she and Sophie didn't get along better, but Sophie hadn't gotten along with the other women, either.

He thought of the dust balls he'd noticed chasing along the hallway of Morgan's house, the cat in her bed, the clothing in a heap on the bedroom floor. Eileen would never tolerate that sort of thing.

And the dog, Major. Strange how he'd forgotten how much Sophie had always wanted a dog. They'd never had one. His wife, Deborah, had been allergic to them.

"Is Sophie home?"

"Yes, she's in her room. She didn't go to school and she wouldn't come down for lunch." The housekeeper's mouth tightened infinitesimally, and then a martyred smile came and went on her handsome features. "We've *both* been listening to her stereo all afternoon, Doctor, and I have to say that infernal racket wears on me. Dinner's been ready for hours, I hope it's not ruined."

She made a point of looking at the man's wristwatch she wore. "I'll just put it on the table for you and then I'll be off, if you don't mind." Eileen was taking computer science at night school at a local college, and Luke wished to God she'd just go to her class without this fussing. It wasn't as if Sophie were a baby or he were helpless.

He thought of Tessa making soup. It would be good for Sophie to learn how to make soup.

"Go on, Eileen. You're late already." He forced a facsimile of a smile. "I think I can manage to get the food from the oven to the table."

"Well, doctor, if you're sure..." Eileen hurried out, and he felt a guilty sense of relief. She was a gem, no doubt about it, but she wasn't relaxing to be around, and tonight he needed to relax.

His chest and stomach felt constricted. He tried for a deep breath and found he couldn't manage one. It stuck somewhere between his chest and stomach. He should start jogging again. A biweekly game of handball kept him fit, but it wasn't enough to really relieve stress. The problem was time, of course, and he spent a great deal of time working.

He needed a drink. He headed for the antique liquor cabinet and poured a healthy dose of Scotch, swallowing a generous mouthful, but it didn't taste as good as he'd expected. Carrying the glass, he climbed the stairs to the second floor, frowning at the muffled rock beat that came from behind Sophie's closed door.

"Sophie, you feeling okay? You're not ill, are you?"

No answer. He paused a moment, undecided, and then hurried along the hall to his own bedroom. He needed to get into comfortable clothing, drink the Scotch, fortify himself before he confronted his daughter. What would Morgan have to say about that, a man who had to drink to face his own daughter?

Twenty minutes later, he and Sophie sat across from each other at the dining table.

"More potatoes?" Luke extended the bowl and frowned when she shook her head. "You've hardly eaten a thing. Eileen said you skipped lunch."

Breakfast, too, undoubtedly. He'd left early, so he hadn't heard her being sick this morning, but he knew the usual routine. It was what had alerted him to her condition. Instead of trying to conceal her sickness, she'd flaunted it until, at six-thirty one morning, he'd finally asked what was wrong with her.

She'd told him, her beautiful gray eyes filled with rebellion, her pretty mouth twisted into a sneer that made him catch his breath in pain and shock.

"What d'you think's wrong, Daddy? I'm pregnant. I sort of thought you'd guess."

The initial rage, the awesome pain and despair he'd felt that morning, three short weeks ago, flared again before he tamped them down.

"Starving yourself won't solve anything, Sophie," he said now. "You'll damage your health, and it'll just make things harder than they already are." He forked up a mouthful of stew and dutifully chewed and swallowed, but the truth was, he didn't have much appetite himself. He pushed his plate away and looked helplessly across at his daughter. He could hear Morgan's voice in his head, like the voice of his conscience.

Get human for once in your life.... Can't you see she needs your reassurance...reassurance...

"We should talk about—" he swallowed and forced the words out of his mouth "—about your pregnancy, Sophie. Your baby. There are issues that need to be decided."

The words swirled in a sick mélange in his head, words like *abortion, private adoption, counseling.* Words he'd used so often, so confidently and calmly in his practice that now had the capacity to make his stomach clench and cold sweat trickle down his forehead.

But Sophie wouldn't speak, wouldn't look at him. Her hair, hanging dank and loose around her shoulders, fell forward to cover most of her face.

"Sophie, please, dear. Ignoring this isn't going to make it go away."

"May-I-*please*-be-excused?"

The childish request reminded Luke of how young she was, both in years and maturity, and how terribly ill equipped she was to face pregnancy and childbirth, much less motherhood.

Motherhood. *Look at the mess I've made of being a father, and I was twenty-five before she was even born.*

"Sophie, have you given any thought to abortion?"

"Abortion?" She looked at him as if he'd suggested incest.

"I've thought this over, and I'm convinced abortion is the best solution. Honey, you're so young, you've got your whole life ahead of you...."

"No." She gave him a look that made him wince. "The answer is no, and that's final. How can you even think of such a thing, Daddy? It's my baby, and Jason's. I'd never get rid of it." She gave him a venomous glare, and then he saw the tears streaming down her cheeks. She swiped at her runny nose with the back of her hand, and his heart contracted with pity and love. His little girl, she was his baby girl....

"Honey, please, don't cry." He reached across to her, but she jerked away, as usual.

"Haven't you done enough harm already, Daddy? You've driv-driven J-Jason away as if my getting preg-pregnant was all his fault." She gulped and struggled to control her voice. "Well, for your information, it wasn't. His fault. I wanted it more than he did. I asked him, I begged him...."

She spat it all out, graphic things he didn't want to know, and Luke gripped the edge of the table, his knuckles white. He couldn't listen to this. It sickened him, thinking of Sophie with that hormone-ridden idiot.

"You had no business threatening Jason that way. You had no right telling him to stay away from me." She was shouting now, out of control. "I *need* him—he's my only friend. I *hate* you for making him go away. I *hate* you, Daddy!"

"Sophie, that's enough," Luke thundered, his patience at an end. "Jason's very fortunate I didn't do more than just yell at him." Damn it, now he'd lost his temper all over again. The very thought of Jason Hendricks having sex with his daughter brought on a killing rage, a fury so overwhelming it terrified him.

Never in all his forty years had he truly believed himself capable of murder. But the confrontation with Jason had taught him that he had depths of rage he'd never tapped. And the fact that Jason was the oldest son of Luke's former best friend seemed both diabolical and cruel. The loss of Adam Hendricks's friendship had left another gaping hole in the rotted fabric his life had become.

Sophie was now sobbing in earnest, bent over

the table, hands over her face, hair trailing in the untouched stew on her dinner plate.

"I...want...my...mummy. I want my mummy," she keened. "If Mom were alive, things would never have turned out this way."

Luke got to his feet. His knees felt weak, his insides churned, and the almost overwhelming need to roar out the truth to his daughter made nausea rise in his throat.

He couldn't, wouldn't tell Sophie that she was partially right. If Deborah were alive, things would indeed be different.

Sophie had no idea that on the day of the car crash that had taken Deborah's life, her mother had been on her way to meet another man, a man with whom she'd been having an affair for some time. Luke had learned the facts only after her death. He, like Sophie, had had no idea that Deborah was leading a double life. She'd been a model housekeeper, gourmet cook, had seemed to be a devoted if less than passionate wife, and all the while she'd been carrying on a torrid affair with someone else.

Feelings of helplessness, hopelessness and utter defeat were beginning to seem like old acquaintances to him. They rolled over him now, as ferocious and inescapable as a tidal wave.

"Your mother's dead, Sophie. You're going

to have to accept that fact and learn to get along with me.''

Sophie's chair crashed backward and toppled to the floor as she ran out of the dining room. He heard her footsteps and her harsh sobs as she flew up the stairs.

The image of a wild-eyed redheaded woman flashed into his mind.

Come down off your high horse and get human for once in your life.

Oh, Morgan. If only you realized just how terribly human I really am, and how inadequate.

AFTER LUKE'S VISIT, Morgan still didn't feel any better. She swallowed the medication he'd left and vomited it up again, wondering between trips to the bathroom what she'd done to deserve such misery. Now she felt guilty for exploding the way she had.

Exhausted, she fell asleep at eight, and sometime during the night the symptoms left as suddenly as they'd appeared. By the next morning she was finally feeling more like herself. She got up and bathed and shampooed her hair and even managed to eat the bowl of tinned peaches and slice of toast Tessa brought her before she left for school.

''You had a phone call last night from Alex Ross. You were dead to the world and I didn't want to wake you, so I told her you had the flu and that you'd call her back when you felt better,'' Tessa told her.

When the girl had hurried off to school, Morgan reached for the bedside phone. Alex was one of her oldest and best friends, and Morgan felt an overwhelming need to talk to her. They'd interned together at St. Joe's and remained close even though Alex and her husband had moved to Korbin Lake, a small town in B.C.'s interior where Cameron ran the local RCMP detachment and Alex had a family practice.

Morgan glanced at the clock as she dialed the familiar number. It was eight-thirty, still early. Alex might not have left for the clinic yet.

Morgan waited through five rings before Alex's harried voice came on the line. In the background was the sound of a child's high-pitched chatter, the banging of dishes and the insistent yowling of a cat.

"Alex, hi. It's me. Have I caught you at a bad time? It sounds as if all hell's breaking loose there. Is that my godson making all that racket?''

"Yup, that's Jonathan all right. He's helping me put the pots and pans away. It always sounds like this around here these days. Hang on while I give Jonnie a cracker and put the cat outside so I can hear you better.'' There was a short pause, and when she came back on the line, Alex said, "My gosh, Morgan, I was worried when Tessa told me you were sick. Is it flu? You're not pregnant or anything exciting like that?"

"Flu, just flu. I'll leave the baby making to you." Morgan cleared her throat. "I'm better this morning, but I've missed several days' work."

"Whew, must be some powerful virus to knock you out of commission. I can't remember you ever missing a day at St. Joe's. I wish I were there to bring you flowers or soup or something. And who's delivering your babies for you?"

Morgan felt a surge of annoyance just thinking about it. "Oh, this insufferable Englishman Jenkins hired behind my back. Yesterday he delivered twins I've been excited about for months, and he sectioned without even giving the mom a chance to do it vaginally. You know how I feel about intervention when it's not strictly necessary."

It felt good to unload her feelings to Alex. "He's been around St. Joe's for a couple years. Maybe you met him when you were in Emerg— Luke Gilbert?"

"Gilbert, Gilbert. Oh yeah. Had all the nurses swooning?"

"That's him."

"Wow, he's a hunk! I only met him a couple

of times, but I thought he was quite nice. Sexy as hell, but he sure wasn't on the make that I could see. He never used his position and good looks to score the way a lot of docs would do.''

Even Morgan had to admit that Luke wasn't a womanizer, but she wasn't about to let that alter her feelings about him.

''He's about the most arrogant man I've ever met,'' she fumed. ''He's the last person I'd ever have chosen to work with. He makes me so uncomfortable I even dread going back to work with him at the clinic.''

''Hey, Morgan, you get along with everybody!'' Alex sounded astonished, and then she added slowly, ''You sure you're not falling for him?''

''For Luke? Oh, phooey, Alex. You know me better than that. Of course I'm not attracted to Luke Gilbert!'' But even as the vehement denial came out of her mouth, Morgan knew with sudden clarity that Alex was right. She was attracted to Luke. She had been from the first moment she'd laid eyes on him. She didn't want to be, she didn't want to face it, but it didn't seem a matter over which she had any control. The knowledge took her breath away and made her slump back weakly on the pillows.

As Tess would say, she had a ''thing'' for Luke Gilbert.

How stupid, how absolutely stupid of her!

CHAPTER FIVE

IT TOOK EVERY OUNCE of Morgan's energy to
change the subject to something safer.

"So, Alex, tell me about you. Are you over
morning sickness yet?" Alex was four months
pregnant, and this second pregnancy had been
rocky from the start.

"I hope so. I realize now how lucky I was
with Jonathan. I hardly had a moment's discomfort until I went into labor. But with this one,
it's been rough, trying to keep up with Jonnie at
home, see patients at work and still have time
with Cam—a little difficult when you're running
off to vomit every ten minutes." Alex's voice
turned thoughtful. "You know, having babies
has changed me, Morgan."

"How so?"

"Well, it's made me a better doctor, for one
thing. I'm more aware now of the pressures on
people, especially women, and how hard it is to
balance work and home and kids and a husband
you love. And it's also made me realize that as
hectic as it all is, I wouldn't trade it for the

world. I know now that I want all those things in my life.''

Morgan listened, and a sudden fierce longing rose in her. What would it be like if Luke loved her, if she was going to have his baby?

Idiot. She was being an idiot.

''I'd be less than whole if I didn't have them,'' Alex was saying. ''Or if I had one thing without the others.''

She paused for a second, obviously belatedly thinking of Morgan's single state, and added in a rush, ''Don't get me wrong here. I'm not suggesting for a minute that everyone should live this way. You need to be half nuts to get into it in the first place. But on the other hand, my friend, don't slam any doors shut before you're really sure that whatever's on the other side isn't something that would make you happy, okay?''

''But I *am* happy,'' Morgan insisted. She was. At least, she had been. Was she at the moment?

Alex made it sound as though love and marriage and children were choices Morgan had deliberately turned down instead of options that had never been viable. And they certainly weren't now.

''Just so you're not cutting off your nose to spite your face with this guy. Ooops.'' There was a huge crash from Alex's end and a furious wail from Jonathan. ''Gotta go, Morgan. Jonnie's upset the high chair on himself. Talk to you soon. Get better quick.''

Morgan hung up the phone, half wishing she'd never made the call in the first place. Admitting to herself that she had some sort of schoolgirl crush on Luke Gilbert was so embarrassing she felt like hiding her head under the covers.

Instead, she slid down, pulled them up to her chin and fell asleep, a long, healing sleep that left her rested and eager to get back to her routine. She also resolved with grim determination to ignore her newfound feelings about Luke Gilbert.

She went back to work the next day, still weak and a little shaky. She was dreading her first encounter with Luke, but she also wanted to get it over with. The memory of her tirade mortified her, and she was going to have to apologize.

They met during office hours that afternoon, and it wasn't all that bad. She might have known his perfect manners would prevail.

"I'm glad you're well again, Morgan" was all he said when they both came into the coffee room. His voice was cool and remote.

"Luke, I'm sorry for the things I said when you came to the house. I'm a rotten patient and I was rude. I apologize."

His half smile didn't quite reach his eyes.

"All doctors are bad patients, Morgan. Don't give it another thought."

She was pitifully grateful that he didn't dwell on the outrageous things she'd said, but a tiny part of her wished he'd be a little more friendly. He poured a cup of coffee and was on his way out of the room with it when he paused and added, "If you have a few moments after work, we need to discuss schedules and rotations."

"Of course," she agreed, and when they met in the reception area late that day, they had a businesslike discussion. Luke discussed office hours, on-call schedules and asked a few questions about some of her patients he'd seen while she was away, and that was that.

Again, Morgan felt let down. She scurried off as soon as things were settled, and as the days passed, she told herself she didn't really need to have much to do with Luke, which was a blessing, considering how she felt. In fact, they hardly saw each other most of the time; they were frantic during office hours and rarely ended up on St. Joe's obstetrical floor at the same time.

As days turned into weeks, Morgan realized that there was no question that having Luke on staff at Women's Place made an enormous difference to the workload. She actually had three consecutive days off during her second week back at work, something that hadn't happened in the entire year she'd worked there.

It was sheer heaven. She had time to hire a carpenter to rebuild the back stairs, and while she was at it, she also hired a cleaning service to shovel the house out on a biweekly basis. Weird, how she only began to really notice the dust and disorder after Luke's disastrous visit. It was almost as if she were beginning to see things through his eyes, God forbid.

She even reluctantly phoned her mother in Florida, realizing she hadn't heard from her for several months. The number rang five times, and then her mother's answering machine clicked on.

"India Merriweather. I'm out at the moment, so please leave your number and I'll return your call." The voice was husky, deep and dramatic. Morgan reflected that she had inherited her voice, if little else, from her mother. She left a brief message and hung up, feeling both relieved and guilty. Conversations with India, rare as they were, never failed to upset her. Well, she'd done her duty. India could return the call or not, as she chose.

Morgan and Tessa also finished the room they were preparing for the baby. They'd papered it in a rainbow pattern, and now they assembled the wooden crib Morgan had bought and filled the drawers of the small white dresser with the baby clothes Morgan's friends at St. Joe's had given them.

"It's the best baby's room ever, isn't it, Morgan? Kyla Jean's gonna be so happy in here." That night Tessa sat for a long time beside the crib in the armless rocking chair Morgan had found at an antique store, rocking back and forth, her eyes soft and filled with dreams.

Touched by the picture she made, Morgan paused in the hallway and stood silently watching for a moment, imagining how marvelous it was going to be, having a baby in the house. Her eyes rested on the compact mound beneath Tessa's black sweatshirt.

It wouldn't be long now.

TWO DAYS LATER, Morgan was slumped on the sofa, catching up on back issues of medical journals. Tessa had made lasagna for dinner, and Morgan felt pleasantly full and more than a little sleepy.

Tessa had been talking on the phone upstairs, and now she came down, slipping her arms into the oversize black leather jacket Morgan had bought her for her birthday.

"Dylan's coming to pick me up. We're going to the vampire movie at the Roxy. That's okay with you, eh, Morgan?" Tessa had experimented with peroxide that afternoon, and now her purple hair had startling canary yellow streaks.

"Try to get home before midnight, Tess. You look tired, sweetie. You need more rest now that you're in your last trimester." It was as close as Morgan dared come to flatly telling the girl to stay home.

Tessa gave her an impish grin. "You're the one with bags under your eyes, Morgan. Three babies in two nights is pushing it. You oughta tell your patients to time things better."

"If only," Morgan agreed fervently. "But I'm going to have an early night tonight." She yawned, and yawned again, aware that she still hadn't regained her usual energy after the bout of flu. She'd caught herself nodding off with her head on her desk that afternoon when she was trying to update charts.

Charts, her nemesis. She'd brought home a stack, and she really ought to be working on them right now. Rachel, the office nurse, had made some pointed comments about how efficient Dr. Gilbert was in keeping charts up to date.

Darn Rachel, anyway. She'd discovered that such remarks brought out every one of Morgan's defenses, as well as her competitive spirit. When it came to the job, whatever Luke could do, Morgan had vowed she could do better.

Except look drop-dead handsome every day of the week, Morgan conceded with a little smile. She couldn't help but notice how sexy he looked in his elegant clothing.

"You going to be warm enough in that dress?" Tessa was wearing a short, loose purple dress over green tights.

"Warm enough? I'm roasting," Tessa said. "Maybe I don't even need this jacket. I just showered and already I feel sticky again." She patted her forehead, careful not to disturb her makeup.

"It's not that warm out, Tess. It's October and the nights are cool. Your baby speeds up your metabolism and makes you feel warmer than normal. Take your jacket along."

"So it's Miss Kyla who's makin' me sweat." Tessa grinned and placed her palm on her stomach, bending her head to talk to her baby. "Yer hot stuff already, kid." She slung the jacket over her arm and said to Morgan, "I'm gonna wait for Dylan on the porch—it's cooler out there."

Morgan was silent as Tessa went outside, wishing she could say, "Stay home with me, Tess. Don't go roaring off on that dratted bike with that irresponsible young thug."

A few moments later Morgan heard the sound of the bike in the drive. Dylan called Tess, and then the bike roared away.

Morgan scowled. Knowing Tessa was clinging to Dylan's back on a motorcycle wasn't a
reassuring thought at all, but then, nothing about
Dylan was reassuring.

She went back to her reading, but soon she
realized she'd scanned the same paragraph three
times and still couldn't say what the article was
about. She tossed the journal to the floor, wishing that Tessa had come with a guidebook.

It was so difficult to know what was best to
do about Dylan. Tessa fancied herself in love
with him. He'd fathered her baby, although he
refused point-blank to attend prenatal classes or
have anything to do with the birth. He'd told
Morgan flatly that he wasn't coming to the hospital when "it" was born, either. He wasn't *into*
that sort of stuff. He'd told Tess to get rid of it,
he'd added with a casual cruelty that had made
Morgan want to slap him.

Obnoxious as she found him, however, Morgan still understood the appeal he had for Tessa.
At seventeen, Dylan was tall and strong, with
well-developed muscles in his shoulders and
torso, and he had unruly black hair that he wore
wild and long. Physically, he was a strikingly
handsome young man, but in Morgan's opinion,
it was a definite case of looks only being skin-
deep.

Tessa had related a few scant facts about Dylan, but Tessa's social worker, Frannie Myles, had filled in lots more.

He lived off and on with his mother in a controlled housing unit on the east side; he'd quit school in grade seven; he worked part-time in a pool hall and spent the rest of his time hanging out with a street gang. He'd already had several minor arrests for shoplifting and stealing hubcaps. Frannie figured he used pot for sure, maybe something more, but at least there was no indication of him dealing drugs.

Alarming as they were, none of those things would have made Morgan dislike him as much as she did if she hadn't glanced through a window when, thinking himself unobserved, he'd kicked out viciously at Skippy as the little dog danced around him. Worst of all, though, was the domineering way he treated Tessa.

She'd had countless heated discussions with Tess about him, to no avail. Tessa was only fifteen, but she was both older and younger than her years. She'd been abandoned at a women's shelter at three months of age, and she'd been in five different foster homes over the years. None of them were terrible, but none had been wonderful, either, and at thirteen the girl began to act out her anger when the couple she'd lived with for three years suddenly divorced, leaving her homeless once again.

She dropped out of school, ran away from the group home she was placed in and lived on the street for eight months, during which time she'd met Dylan. He became her protector, in return for sex, of course.

To Tessa he was her knight in shining armor.

Fortunately, Tessa also met Frannie Myles during her time on the street. Frannie was a social worker at the hospital, and she did volunteer work at a teen shelter on weekends. She was touched by Tessa's vivacity and her determined optimism. When Tessa became pregnant, Frannie had enlisted Morgan's help in convincing the young girl that an abortion was the best and only choice, but the attempt backfired.

During Tessa's first appointment, Morgan's heart went out to the girl. She listened to Tessa explaining that she wanted and needed to have her baby, that given the chance she'd go back to school, finish her education, turn her life around, whatever it took. She loved dolls, she confided with heart-wrenching naiveté, and she wanted her baby more than she'd ever wanted anything in her life.

Morgan believed her. There was a determination in Tessa that Morgan admired, and as she'd done a thorough physical on Tessa's thin body that spring afternoon, she'd really listened to the girl, and something inside of her responded.

Morgan had her huge house, which was pretty much empty if you discounted the animals. She adored babies, although she'd reluctantly admitted several years before that she probably wouldn't be having any of her own. She'd considered single parenthood and decided against it. She knew better than anyone how much children needed two parents, and she wouldn't deliberately do that to a child.

She had no experience with teenagers, but what the heck, they were people, weren't they? She'd learn.

So, against almost everyone's advice, Morgan opened her home and her heart to Tessa. The girl responded with enthusiasm, studying with a tutor so she could enter the special classes the school board offered for pregnant teens, showing Morgan in every way how grateful she was. The only real misgivings Morgan had ever had were over Dylan.

Well, Doc, what can you do to change the situation? she asked herself now, as she had so many times in the past five months. And the answer, certainly for the moment, was not a darned thing.

She'd talked it over countless times with Frannie, and they'd agreed that if Morgan for-

bade Tessa to see Dylan, all the girl's issues
about security, love, protection and freedom
would surface, and Morgan knew the tenuous
bond she and Tess shared wasn't yet strong
enough to withstand such a confrontation.

So if you can't change it, accept it, she reminded herself now, trying to put her nagging
uneasiness about Tessa out of her mind.

To heck with the charts. She'd have a long,
hot bath and go to bed, she decided.

LUKE WAS IN his study plowing through a stack
of charts when Eileen tapped at the door and
then stuck her head in, her eyes big behind her
glasses, her voice lowered to a conspirational
whisper. "Adam Hendricks is in the living
room. He says to tell you he won't leave without
talking to you."

Adam. Luke hadn't seen or spoken to his
friend since the day he'd found out Sophie was
pregnant by Adam's son. That meeting had been
explosive. As far as Luke was concerned, they
had nothing more to say to each other.

His jaw set in a grim line, he brushed past
Eileen and strode into the living room.

Adam was sitting in an armchair that seemed
too small to hold his huge, muscular frame. He'd
been a football player in his youth, and his job
as a contractor kept him physically fit. He was

dressed casually, as always, his big body threatening to spill out of his worn jeans and checked shirt. He got to his feet when Luke came in, and the two men stood facing one another across the low coffee table, the tension between them thick and palpable.

"Adam." Luke's voice was icy cold. "What can I do for you?" Against his will, he remembered pleasant Saturday afternoons he'd spent with this big, affable man over games of cribbage and glasses of beer, laughing and discussing everything under the sun, and for a moment, the loss of his best friend seemed unbearable.

"I thought maybe we could talk about this mess our kids are in without shouting this time," Adam said, his craggy face solemn. "It's pretty stupid to go on the way we've been doing, don't you figure, Luke? There're practical matters to be considered, things Peggy and I would like to know. After all, this baby will be our grandchild as well as yours."

Even though he still felt murderously angry when he thought of Jason's role in this, Adam was right. It was childish to not speak to each other. Luke sat down and waited.

"This whole thing has caused a lot of upset in our family," Adam began. "The other kids are affected, as well as Jason. We've talked it over with all of them, and what bothers us the most is what's gonna happen to the baby.''

At seventeen, Jason was the oldest of four, with two sisters, twelve and fourteen, and a brother who was only nine. They'd welcomed Sophie into their midst, and Luke remembered with bitter irony how grateful he'd been when Sophie and Jason became friends.

Anger boiled up inside him again, but he subdued it.

"I'm trying to convince Sophie to have an abortion, but at this point she insists she's having the child," he said stiffly. "In that case, a private adoption seems reasonable. I'll be doing my best to convince her of that option." He hadn't really made up his mind, but he said it anyway.

Adam nodded, leaning forward, his hands on his knees, his blue eyes troubled. "Look, if it's a case of adoption, Peggy and I want to raise the baby. None of us could sleep nights thinking it was being raised by strangers."

Luke wasn't sure he could himself, but he didn't say so. Adam waited, and when Luke didn't comment, he said, "This is Jason's kid as much as Sophie's, Luke. I think you're making a big mistake, not allowing him to see her, to take responsibility."

Luke's fists balled, and his voice was hard as

steel. "There's to be no contact whatsoever between them. Nothing will change my mind about that. You can remind Jason that if he were one year older, I'd charge him with statutory rape."

Adam got to his feet. "Damn! I wish you'd stop being such a hard-ass about this, Luke. Jason's young, he's made a serious mistake and he knows it. I'm not making excuses for him, I just figure we've all made mistakes in our lives. You're dead wrong not to let the kids face this together. It would do that boy of mine a lot of good to support Sophie during her pregnancy, to be there when the baby's born."

"Not in my lifetime." Luke gritted out the words between clenched teeth.

Adam shrugged helplessly and shook his head. "Okay, it's your call, but it seems to me Sophie needs all the support she can get right now, and all of us would help out however we could if you'd only let us."

Luke didn't reply.

Adam shook his head in frustration. "By keeping them apart, you're letting Jason off the hook, you know."

"I won't have him around my daughter, and that's final."

"Then I guess there's not much left to say." Adam sighed. "You change your mind at any time, let me know."

The door closed behind him, and Adam was pathetically grateful when the phone rang, summoning him to the hospital to deliver a baby.

MORGAN WAS SLEEPING too deep even for dreams when the phone began to ring. Usually, she was awake and alert in an instant, but this time she couldn't manage it. She finally got her hand around the receiver and mumbled a groggy greeting.

"Morgan? It's Luke. I'm over at St. Joe's—one of my patients just delivered."

Why the heck was he waking her up to tell her that? she wondered in irritation. She squinted at the bedside clock. One forty-five.

"Morgan, they've just brought Tessa Hargraves up from Emerg. Apparently she's had some sort of—" He hesitated, then added, "Some sort of accident."

Morgan came fully awake and made a shocked sound in her throat. "Is she bad?"

"She's not badly injured, but when she arrived her membranes had already ruptured and her cervix is dilated seven centimeters." Concern was evident in the tone of his voice. "She's in advanced active labor and there's strong indication of fetal distress."

Morgan's heart thumped, and sick dread made her stomach hurt.

CHAPTER SIX

"PLEASE, LUKE, tell her I'll be right there."

Morgan could hear his voice as he added something, but she dropped the phone, shoving her legs into jeans and pulling on the shirt she'd worn the night before as her frantic mind tried to make sense of too few facts.

An accident. Probably a motorcycle accident, damn that stupid, irresponsible Dylan!

Not badly hurt, but in premature labor, too far advanced to stop with drugs.

Morgan added swiftly in her head. The baby was thirty weeks. It should be safely past the age of viability, but she knew from ultrasound that the fetus was small—IUGR—intrauterine growth retardation. Tessa's baby needed more time in the womb.

Luke had said there was fetal distress.

They'd need a miracle.

She tore down the stairs and into the garage, and within moments she was in the Jeep, speeding like a demented race-car driver through the quiet Vancouver streets.

At St. Joe's, she ignored the ancient, slow elevators and tore up the stairs. Bursting through the wide doors leading to the delivery rooms, the first thing she heard was the muffled sound of someone screaming hysterically from one of the case rooms, and she knew in her heart it was Tessa.

"Delivery Room 4. Dr. Gilbert's with her." Juliet, the labor room nurse, was always the epitome of calm, but now her huge liquid eyes were somber in her exotic, dark-skinned face. There was no need for her to ask why Morgan was there. All the nurses knew Morgan—the obstetrical team were like her family—and of course they knew all about Tessa.

Feverishly impatient, Morgan pulled on her gloves and opened the case-room door on a scene of controlled chaos. She waited as Juliet tied on her surgical gown, barely able to tolerate the necessary delay. From where she stood she could already see that the monitor showed fetal deceleration, which meant that delivery had to be imminent. The baby was in trouble, and it had to come out fast.

Tessa was hysterical, in the throes of a contraction, wailing as she thrashed around on the short delivery bed. Two nurses, also Morgan's friends, were doing their best to calm her, and

Luke was positioned between her widespread legs.

A neonatal specialist, Aaron Landry, hovered nearby.

Morgan hurried to the table and bent over to whisper to the girl. She'd learned long ago that whispering to patients often forced them to focus outside, instead of being totally caught up with what was happening inside their pain-ravaged bodies.

"Tessa," she breathed. "Tessa, sweetie, I'm here. Now calm down, it's gonna be okay. We're all here to help you, but you have to concentrate and do your job, too. Remember how we talked about this?"

Morgan's whispering at last did the trick, and Tessa turned her head toward her, her eyes wild and pupils dilated, but at least she stopped struggling.

Morgan smiled at her reassuringly, stroking the girl's hair and assessing the damage the accident had done. There was a shallow cut on Tessa's forehead oozing blood, and the thin, bare arm closest to Morgan was scraped raw, with gravel imbedded in the cuts.

What troubled Morgan was Tessa's left eye. The tissue surrounding it and the temple area were already discoloring, but there was no sign of gravel or scraping on her cheek. The eye looked as though it had connected with a fist.

"Mybaaby, mybaaaby. It's too sooon. Pleeease do something, Morgan, pleeease," she keened, and Morgan's heart contracted with pity and love.

"Just work with us here and do as we say. We're all going to help, honey," Morgan instructed her in a calm voice, forcing a reassuring smile. "Keep your eyes open now and stay focused," she said. "That's a good girl. Breathe through this contraction. Breathe, breathe...." Morgan guided Tessa with her own breaths.

"Head's presenting. Next contraction will do it. You've got to push when I say, Tessa," Luke urged, and the words were barely out of his mouth when the next contraction began.

Tessa's eyes bulged with pain and panic and strain, and Morgan continued to talk quietly into her ear.

"That's it, sweetie. Push into your bum now as if you're having a big BM. Good girl. Push now, push...."

"Push, push, push." The entire team joined in the litany, and with deceptive slowness, the tiny head appeared, rotated, paused, and then in one bloody rush, Tessa's daughter was born.

She was alive but impossibly tiny, flaccid and grey, dangerously still. Luke clamped the cord with deft fingers and handed her swiftly to Aaron, but Morgan had seen enough babies to know when there was little hope. This little girl was flat.

A Code 333 went out, the emergency code that meant a baby was dying, and Aaron raced with her to an adjoining room where specialists would try everything medical science had to offer in an effort to save her.

Tessa was frantic. "Is she okay? Where did they take her? Why didn't she cry? Is my baby okay, Morgan? Please, please let my baby be okay."

Tessa's agonized voice tore at every single nerve cell. Morgan struggled to keep her tone optimistic. "We're trying, honey. We're doing everything we can."

But at last Aaron came back in and shook his head, and the silence in the room brought an agonizing, endless scream from Tessa. She knew her baby was gone.

MORGAN WAS THE ONE who tenderly bathed the tiny body, dressed her in a white sleeper, wrapped her in a soft blanket and took her in to Tessa.

Morgan had also performed the nurse's painful task of taking pictures of the baby, recording hand and footprints, snipping a lock of the silky fair hair. The pain in her heart was terrible, but she damped down her own sorrow, wanting only to do whatever she could for Tessa and for the precious little girl that would never grow.

At first, Tessa was frightened when Morgan brought the baby in, but Morgan laid the small, still bundle in Tessa's arms and encouraged her to look at her daughter, knowing that Tessa needed to hold her, even give her the name she'd chosen, Kyla Jean. Tessa couldn't properly grieve for a baby she'd never seen or held, and Morgan knew that grieving was essential if the girl was to recover from this tragedy.

With shaking fingers Tessa drew the blanket back and looked down at her daughter's face. Ever so slowly, she laid her on her lap and unwrapped the blanket.

"She's beautiful, just the way I knew she'd be," Tessa said, and Morgan's heart felt as if it were breaking.

The nurses kept holy water, and together Morgan and Tessa stroked a few drops across Kyla's minute forehead, naming her. The pastor from Morgan's church would come and formally baptize her, but the private little ceremony was comforting.

Morgan stayed at Tessa's side while the girl held her baby. Tessa didn't cry. Instead, she examined Kyla's tiny, perfect hands and feet, admired the shock of golden hair on her well-shaped skull.

Morgan noted that Tessa didn't once ask for Dylan or even mention him. Morgan had slipped out for an instant and asked Juliet to see if Dylan had been with Tessa when she was admitted to Emerg. Juliet confirmed that there'd been no sign of him. Tessa had been brought in alone, by ambulance.

When Tessa as last agreed to allow Juliet to take away the baby, Morgan sat holding the girl's hand as she gradually succumbed to the mild sedative Luke had ordered. She still didn't cry, and as the drug took hold, Morgan finally risked asking the necessary questions.

She stroked the girl's hair and forehead with gentle hands, her voice soft.

"What happened tonight, honey? Dr. Gilbert said you had an accident. Did you fall from the motorcycle?" Morgan needed to know the truth. "Can you tell me how it happened, Tess?"

Tessa nodded, her eyes fluttering shut, and Morgan felt her shudder. "I fell, not off the bike, though. Down these cem-cement steps, at the side of the theater. Dylan was having a smoke there."

Morgan gently touched the puffy eye, now turning black and blue. "And is that how you got this, falling down the steps?"

Tessa hesitated, tears at last sliding out from beneath her closed lids before she slowly nodded, and Morgan, sick at her soul, knew she was lying.

"Dylan hit you, didn't he, sweetie?" Morgan had to make Tessa acknowledge the awful truth.

Tessa's face crumpled and now the tears began in earnest. "We...had a fight. He didn't mean for me to fall, I know he didn't. He kept saying he was sorry." She sobbed weakly, and Morgan tenderly used a cold cloth on her eyes and cheeks, but she was filled with such a tremendous fury her hands trembled.

Tessa at last slid into exhausted sleep, and Morgan made her way to the staff lounge and slumped down on the old couch, gradually allowing the utter exhaustion and the terrible sorrow she'd held at bay for hours to finally claim her. The events of the past few hours had been painful beyond belief, and she'd had to subdue her own feelings so as to comfort and help Tessa.

Now, those suppressed emotions rose to the surface, and Morgan began to tremble. The memory of the perfect, delicate little baby's body brought a sob to her throat, and she bent forward, head on her knees, and opened her mouth wide, crying aloud for the baby who'd never had a chance to live.

She sobbed and gulped and choked, aware
that she was making a terrible noise and not caring. After a long while, the pain eased a tiny bit
and the trembling subsided.

Her eyes were still streaming and she needed
to blow her nose. She lifted her head to look for
a box of tissue and realized Luke was standing
just inside the door. She hadn't heard him come
in, and she didn't have energy enough to even
care whether or not he'd witnessed her grief.

Silently, he reached into his trousers pocket
and handed her an ironed and carefully folded
white linen handkerchief.

Too drained to politely refuse, Morgan took
it and wiped her eyes. It didn't seem right to
blow her nose on such pristine splendor, but she
did anyway, twice.

"Thanks," she said, her voice thick and
hoarse with crying, her words catching in her
throat. "I've lost them before, but this is the
worst I've ever had to go through. It...it feels
like losing my own baby. Oh, Luke, I never get
used to it. Do you?"

He didn't ask what she meant. His face was
somber, and he shook his head slowly. "No. I
never do, either. I can't believe anyone could.
Losing a baby, or a mother, is my worst nightmare. What happened in there—" He sank down

on the sofa beside her, hands clasped between his knees, head bent so his dark hair fell forward.

"She...she was such a beau-beautiful baby, such a perfect little girl, wasn't she?" Morgan could feel sobs rising inside her all over again, and she pressed a hand to her mouth to try to choke them back, but they erupted anyway, and she cried helplessly, hands pressed to her burning face.

"She *was* beautiful. Oh, God, I'm so sorry, Morgan. Bloody hell, I'm so sorry."

Through the choking sobs and the tears, she felt his strong hand on her back, rubbing clumsily back and forth in a soothing rhythm, and her devastation was so great that she turned instinctively toward him, aching for simple human comfort. She rested her head on his shoulder and let her heartbreak run its course, using his handkerchief to blot her eyes and blow her nose again.

That was when she realized with utter shock that she wasn't the only one crying. She was so surprised her own tears dried, and she lifted a tentative hand to touch his wet, rough cheek.

Luke Gilbert, cool, remote, always composed, was struggling to maintain some remnant of control, but his eyes were streaming, the muscles in his throat and jaw working feverishly to subdue what he was feeling.

He swore viciously and screwed his eyes shut, and then a wordless sound of utter agony burst from his throat as he buried his face in his hands.

His desolation pierced Morgan like an arrow. She wrapped her arms tightly around him, the natural healer in her needing to give comfort, to ease the awful pain that must have given rise to that terrible sound, this awful grief.

She could feel his entire body trembling convulsively, and then his strong arms came around her in one quick desperate motion, sweeping her close against his chest and holding her there, clutching her so hard she could barely breathe.

For an instant, she was enveloped in an embrace familiar to her from countless half-remembered dreams. He smelled clean, of hospital soap and some pleasant kind of aftershave. He was all corded muscle and sinewy strength. She felt the quivering of nerves tensed to withstand the barrage of emotion, and she was aware of a raw physical power in his large body that the elegance of his clothing concealed.

He gained control of himself at last. For one long, heart-stopping moment, she felt him press his face into her hair. Unable to resist, she raised a hand and touched his cheek, noting the faint roughness of his beard, the elegant bones beneath the skin.

At her touch, he disengaged himself gently

and pulled away. He leaned against the back of
the sofa, head tipped back, eyes closed. He drew
in a long, shuddering breath, then blurted,
"Morgan, my daughter, Sophie, is pregnant."

Morgan couldn't have been more surprised.
She gaped at him, unable to say a word, and he
continued in a flat, ragged tone. "She's about
Tessa's age, only a baby herself, and... Oh,
damn it all, Morgan, damn it to hell, I simply
don't know what to do! I'm alone with her, I'm
bloody useless as a parent—"

Anguish tinged his voice. "She isn't even
speaking to me at the moment, I don't seem to
be able to say anything to her that doesn't cause
a row."

Morgan continued to stare at him, stunned
speechless. When she found her voice, she could
only stammer, "Oh, L-Luke, I'm s-so awfully
sorry." Suddenly many of his actions took on a
whole different meaning. "How...how far along
is she?" The practical query masked the waves
of shock and shame Morgan was feeling over
the way she'd judged him.

"Fifteen weeks."

"Fifteen weeks. Nearly four months," Morgan repeated, feeling stupid. She couldn't seem
to make her brain work; she couldn't think what
to say to help him. Over the past weeks, she'd
constructed an elaborate, harsh persona for Luke

in her imagination, trying to talk herself out of the emotions he aroused in her. Now, in these few moments, he was demonstrating how very wrong she'd been.

She was ashamed, mortified at her own selfish interpretation of what she now realized must have been a superhuman effort on his part to conceal terrible anxiety.

"Four months—there's still time for an abortion. Is she considering that option?" Morgan detested the procedure but had to acknowledge the practical necessity in certain cases.

Luke shook his head. "I suggested it, of course." He shrugged helplessly. "She refused point-blank. She won't hear of it. She insists she wants to have the child."

"Yes, I understand. Tessa was exactly the same." From the pain in his eyes, Morgan guessed that the suggestion and the resulting discussion hadn't been as rational as the tone in which Luke recounted it. She felt terrible for him, and she also felt helpless.

She reached out to touch his strong hand with her fingers. "I believe it's a decision a girl must make herself, no matter how young she is, even though it impacts the lives of those around her. As I said, Tessa was absolutely determined to have…her baby. And to keep it, raise it."

Morgan's voice wobbled and broke as tears

once again trickled from her eyes. "And I wanted that so much, as well, I wanted to help her. I love babies. I was looking forward to watching her grow, being sort of...an auntie," she added, once again absently wiping her eyes and nose with Luke's crumpled handkerchief. She regained control of herself and blew her nose fiercely. It was sore and undoubtedly fiery red, but that didn't matter.

When she was done, Luke reached over and covered her hand with his, his voice filled with misery.

"In my mind, I've gone over and over every part of this delivery, trying to think what else I might have done, whether there was anything I didn't do that I should have."

Morgan was appalled. "Don't. Oh, please, Luke, don't second-guess this. Don't do that to yourself." She was all too familiar with the feelings of uncertainty and self-doubt an obstetrician suffered when a tragedy occurred in the delivery room. "You did everything humanly possible. We all did. You know as well as I do that some babies just aren't meant to live."

He was silent for a long time, still holding her hand, smoothing his thumb slowly across her knuckles, back and forth. At last, in a quiet voice, he said, "Someone hit Tessa, didn't they?

It was obvious to me that she'd been punched in the eye."

"Dylan." Morgan spat out the name. "The father of her baby." She was suddenly breathing hard, her anger and outrage making her tremble all over again. "From what Tessa said, I gather there was a fight. He punched her, and she fell down a flight of stairs."

Suddenly Morgan bent over, gasping, as though she felt the blow herself.

Luke's grip tightened painfully on her hand, and he cursed, a string of words Morgan would never have imagined him using. "Can you convince her to press charges?"

Morgan hadn't asked Tessa. There was no need. She already knew the answer and she shook her head.

"She won't. I know that without asking. She believes she loves him. He'll convince her it was really her fault, not his."

"Familiar story." Luke sighed, and Morgan nodded. Both of them, during their years as physicians, had all too often treated women who were abused, and they knew the pattern, the denial, the subtle shifting of blame to the victim.

"You'll make certain she doesn't see him again, however." It wasn't a question. His voice was filled with conviction. "She's only fifteen, so as her foster parent you can do that, can't you?''

"Nope." Morgan shook her head and sighed. "It doesn't work like that. I'd like to murder Dylan, and at this moment, I feel capable of it. I'll certainly tell him exactly what I think of him, but whether she sees him or not is entirely Tessa's decision."

Luke released her hand and gave her a surprised and decidedly judgmental look. "That's certainly a liberal view."

Morgan gave a tired shrug. "It's the way things are. I knew how it was with Dylan before Tessa came to live with me. I don't like it, but I can't change it at the moment, so I have to accept what is."

He scowled. "Well, I wish I saw things as clearly as you do, Morgan. With Sophie, it seems I react first and reason later."

Once again, compassion for him filled her, and she wanted to comfort him. "It's different for you—you've been with Sophie since she was born. You're her father, so naturally you can't be objective. I'm not Tessa's natural parent, and it's really too late for me to be her foster mother." Her tone was wistful. "All I can try to do is be her friend."

A ghost of a smile flitted across his features. "She's a very fortunate girl, then, because it seems to me you have a rare and particular gift for friendship, Morgan.''

The unexpected compliment, the first personal one he'd ever paid her, sent a wave of warmth right through her, and she flushed and couldn't look at him. It felt as if he'd given her something precious just when she needed it most, and his words eased some of her pain.

CHAPTER SEVEN

"THE STAFF HERE at St. Joe's will do anything for you," Luke told Morgan. "And I've learned to my chagrin that almost every single one of your patients regards you as her close personal friend. They tolerate me when you're not around, but it's quite clear that they prefer you."

Morgan was flustered and then defensive. "I know you probably feel I'm not professional enough, that I don't maintain the proper distance between physician and patient."

It was a familiar criticism, one she'd weathered throughout her internship and residency.

"I thought so at first. Now I only envy your easy manner, your knack for making friends." He got to his feet, his hands thrust in the pockets of his pants, and started pacing up and down the room. "God knows I could use some of your charm myself. I can't even talk to my own daughter."

Again the raw pain in his voice touched Morgan's heart. She got to her feet and put her hand on his arm, forcing him to stop and look at her as she searched for something to say that wouldn't sound like empty platitudes or gratuitous advice.

She looked up at him, straight into the eyes she'd always thought were hard and green and cold. Now she saw the vulnerability and desolation there.

"Luke, you love her. I'm certain she knows that. When you care about someone, there's always a way to work things through." Morgan's mind was racing, searching for a practical suggestion. "Look, there's a counselor here at St. Joe's Tessa likes. Frannie Myles. Maybe you know her?"

"I've met her, yes."

"Well, Frannie's great with kids. She's young and she likes teenagers. She seems to have a real rapport with them. Maybe it would help if you and Sophie talked to her?" she added before she could think better of it.

"I think not." The refusal was immediate. "Frankly, the hospital gossip mill scares the hell out of me. I despise the thought of everyone discussing my daughter and her personal problems. I've overheard enough intimate conversations in the cafeteria to know it happens."

Morgan knew he was right about gossip. She felt heat flush her chest and neck and stain her cheeks. She remembered all too well how many

times she herself had listened avidly to some tid-
bit of information about him, and again, she felt
ashamed of herself.

"Frannie would never betray a confidence,"
she insisted. "And," she added stiffly, "I hope
you realize everything we've said here is confidential. I certainly won't breathe a word. I
wouldn't dream of—"

He shocked her by reaching out and gripping
her shoulders. He gave her a tiny shake. "Don't
go all huffy on me again, Morgan, all right? I
like it much better when you're not glaring and
hollering and making well-deserved remarks
about my bedside manner."

Morgan looked up at him in amazement. Unless she really had her wires crossed, he was
actually teasing her! He wasn't quite smiling,
but there was humor in his tone and gentle
amusement in his green eyes. For the first time
in hours, she tried to smile, and though her face
felt stiff from tears, it felt wonderful.

Luke still had hold of her shoulders and didn't
seem about to let go. He was staring down into
her eyes, and the intensity of his gaze mesmer-
ized her.

She'd really been mistaken about his eyes.
There was nothing cool about them. At this moment, they seemed to burn, and the heat seared
her soul.

HE KNEW HE OUGHT to let her go, but Luke couldn't seem to release her. He held her lightly, aware of the fragility of her small bones and the contrasting strength of her nature. A warmth radiated from her that he couldn't resist, a warmth both physical and emotional, and with shocking suddenness his sexuality, dormant for so long, reared to life with a ferocity that rocked him to his very depths.

This tiny woman with the riotous red curls and shiny tear streaks all over her smooth cheeks, this stubborn person with the melting chocolate brown gaze and full lips devoid of any lipstick— This wasn't at all the sort of woman that he ought to be attracted to, a small, puzzled voice in his brain reminded him.

He'd always liked statuesque, serene women, quiet spoken and self-possessed, with an aura of dignity and a quality of mystery about them.

This little spitfire who opened her mouth square and wide and howled her grief out like an injured child, who took offense between one breath and the next...this person wasn't any of the things he'd always thought he wanted in a woman.

Soft, warm, small. Drawn by something he couldn't name and didn't recognize, driven by a need more powerful than even his need for self-control, he slowly bent over her, moving his hands upward from her shoulders and cupping her face between his palms, delighted by the satiny smoothness of her skin. He liked the way she smelled, a natural scent entirely her own.

She gulped and drew in a ragged breath through opened lips, and before she could expel it, he bent his head and kissed her, noting that she didn't close her eyes the way he'd expected. Instead, they remained wide open, alarmed, huge, until her features blurred in his vision. He closed his own eyes, and a shock of intense feeling replaced sight.

Her lips were full and soft and startled. She tasted a little salty, of tears and stale coffee, and also of something wild and bittersweet, like berries ripened in sunshine. Her hands came up and rested on his chest, not pushing him away, and he fought the impulse to lift her small body from the floor and crush her tight against him. Her mouth was lush, and he explored it with tongue and teeth and urgent hunger.

She made a sound in her throat of pleasure and need, and slowly her arms encircled his chest until she was holding him, pressing against him, making him painfully aware of full, soft breasts and a small but well-shaped body.

When at last he forced himself to draw away, his trembling hands slid down the sides of her head to her throat. She had a lovely throat, slender, smooth, long. He put a thumb on each side, over the arteries, and at first all he could feel was his own blood hammering through his veins, but then Morgan's heartbeat drummed a vibrant, visible echo.

Now her eyes were closed, and they stayed closed as each of them struggled to control their breathing. She swayed and he steadied her, and at last she opened her eyes and looked up at his face, shell-shocked and dazed.

"Holy *toot*," she drawled in her deep, resonant voice. "What was *that* all about?"

It was so typically Morgan, so irreverent and unexpected and honest, that it made him grin. "I'm not quite sure. Call it an irresistible impulse."

She frowned up at him as if she'd never really seen him before. "But why did you kiss *me?*" She made it sound as if the room were full of other women, all ready and willing, and her ingenuous query startled him.

He found himself telling her the truth. "It suddenly dawned on me that you're a very lovely woman, Morgan."

To his amazement, she was instantly angry. She twisted away from his hands, her face flushed. She scowled up at him, hands on her hips, husky voice hard-edged. "That's a load of crap and you know it. You...you just felt sorry for me, didn't you?''

He gaped down at her, and it occurred to him that she was insecure about herself as a woman, unaware of her appeal, her sexuality. The realization stunned him. She'd always seemed so confident, so self-assured. Her vulnerability touched him, and instead of withdrawing, as his instincts prompted when this volatile woman was in one of her tempers, he stepped toward her and caught both her hands in a firm grip.

She struggled for a moment and then was still, but she wouldn't look at him. Her cheeks were hot and her hands were cold and trembling.

''Listen to me, Morgan. I don't go around kissing my co-workers because I feel sorry for them.'' He put all the intensity he was feeling into his words. ''I don't kiss anyone unless I very much want to, and I suspect that's true for you, as well.'' He looked down into a tumble of curly red hair, which was all he could see of her because she was staring at her feet like a stubborn child.

Amusement tinged his voice. ''Besides, I think you'd probably have given me a bloody nose if I tried kissing you against your will. You're not exactly a shrinking...sunflower.'' No one in their right mind would compare Morgan to a violet.

The door to the lounge burst open and two physicians came in, their voices raised in a heated discussion about someone's intestines.

Luke let her go, and the moment he did, Morgan spun on her heel and hurried out of the room without another word.

Feeling both excited and drained, Luke went into the washroom and splashed his face with cold water. He had a locker where he kept a clean shirt, and he retrieved it and put it on, along with his tweed sport jacket. He had patients to see, charts to sign, and after that, office hours at the clinic. But as the morning progressed, he realized his attention wasn't on the job.

He'd always been adept at putting his personal life on hold, shoving disturbing issues into another part of his mind and locking the door so he could get on with his work. Countless times, he'd used the technique to keep himself from feeling things he didn't want to feel.

This morning, however, the door to that locked room in his head refused to stay closed, and tactile images of Morgan flashed through his consciousness, memories of how she'd felt in his arms and how urgently his body had reacted.

He stared down unseeingly at the chart the charge nurse on maternity handed him.

"Dr. Gilbert?"

Luke looked at her, realizing that she'd said something to him, and he didn't have any idea what it was.

"Are you all right, Doctor?"

"Yes. Yes, of course. I'm just fine. Now, what were you saying about Mrs. Ellington?"

"She has a slightly elevated temp and some discharge and cramping."

He couldn't make sense of the ordinary words. He wasn't fine at all, and he knew it. It felt to Luke as if still another portion of his life had broken away from the well-ordered pattern he'd always struggled to maintain. It had gone sailing off into unknown and frightening territory—Morgan Jacobsen's volatile and disorganized territory, to be exact.

And that scared him to death.

CHAPTER EIGHT

"ASHES TO ASHES, dust to dust."

The minute white coffin with its blanket of pink rosebuds was lowered into the wet earth, and Morgan scrubbed away the steady tears that mingled with the raindrops this wet early morning.

Kyla Jean Hargraves was being laid to rest in the old cemetery situated only a few short blocks from Morgan's house. Tessa had requested that her daughter be buried there. "I feel closer to her that way. I can walk over sometimes and say 'Hi,'" Tessa declared, and Morgan felt as if her heart were breaking.

But she also felt supported in that heartbreak. When she'd arranged with the pastor for this early-morning service, she'd thought that she and Tessa and Frannie Myles and perhaps one or two friends would be the only ones there, but she was deeply touched and grateful to find that most of the nurses not on duty at St. Joe's came, as well as several of the people who worked at Women's Place. Floral tributes abounded, and

Morgan felt humbled by the evidence of friendship and caring.

In spite of her sadness, her heart had skipped a beat when she walked into the chapel and saw that Luke was there, his dark head towering over the women seated around him.

Morgan hadn't seen him since their encounter in the hospital lounge. She'd relived the kiss they'd shared time and again, trying to make sense of it, waking at night with the feel of it on her lips, her body burning with sexual reaction.

It was both comforting and disturbing to have him in the chapel, and she'd felt disappointment as well as relief when his beeper sounded halfway through the service. He'd slipped out the door, catching her eye for an instant and giving her an apologetic shake of his head and a tiny salute.

Dylan Vogler, on the other hand, was conspicuous by his absence. Morgan didn't think there'd been any contact between Tessa and him since the baby's birth. She'd seen Tessa's desperate gaze sweep over the small assembly in the tiny chapel, obviously searching for her baby's father and not finding him. Her face had crumpled for a moment, but she hadn't cried. She was pale and shaky, but composed and strangely dignified as the painful service began.

Tessa seemed to have grown years older in

the five days since her baby's birth and death, and Morgan felt an overwhelming surge of compassion, love and protectiveness for this fragile girl-woman in her care.

Morgan tracked Dylan down herself late that evening. She caught up with him in a pool hall, where he was surrounded by leering, foul-mouthed friends. She had to exert monumental control to stop herself from physically attacking him. She told him in vivid detail about his baby's untimely birth and death, and she made it clear she held him fully accountable.

"If Tessa would agree, I'd have you charged with assault, as well as the murder of your daughter," she spat at him, ignoring the jeering of his pals.

"Yeah? Well, Doc, it ain't none of your business, is it, what goes on between my lady and me." But for a moment, Morgan saw fear in his eyes, and she was glad.

"You gonna go around making threats, maybe you better watch your back, bitch," Dylan snarled, and her hand ached to slap his leering face.

Morgan turned then and walked out, trembling so hard she could barely even drive home.

She could only hope that the baby's death at least meant that Dylan was gone from Tessa's life for good.

TESSA INSISTED on returning to school just two days after the funeral. Morgan was worried about her. Tessa was remote and quiet, and she wasn't eating.

Morgan tried several times to get the girl to talk with her about the tragic events that had led up to the baby's birth and how she felt about Dylan's role in the whole thing, but Tessa was stubbornly silent. All Morgan could think to do was talk to Frannie Myles and ask her advice.

She tracked the counselor down in her tiny office at St. Joe's, charmed as always by the younger woman's warm manner. Frannie was tall, slender and striking, with long golden brown hair drawn into a tight knot on her neck, and eyes of a deep, calm blue. She had the fluid grace of a dancer and the crooked smile of a mischievous child.

She wasn't smiling now. Like Morgan, she was concerned about Tessa.

"I'm afraid she's blaming herself for her baby's death. It's exactly what Dylan's taught her to do, to take on guilt for his actions," Morgan confided to Frannie.

"We'll just have to give her time to grieve in her own way," Frannie said in her quiet voice. "Actually, I've started a group I'd like Tessa to join, girls from all over the city dealing with various aspects of teenage pregnancy and motherhood, as well as loss. Several of them have given babies up for adoption, and one girl lost her child to cancer. Maybe Tessa could talk about her feelings with them easier than she can with you and me.''

Morgan agreed, and she thought of Luke's daughter.

"I have a friend whose kid is pregnant, same age as Tess. Would you mind if I mentioned the group to him?''

"Please do. She'd be very welcome.''

MORGAN HADN'T SEEN Luke except in passing since the funeral, and she felt both shy and nervous about talking to him. She glimpsed him loping down the corridor ahead of her later that afternoon at St. Joe's, and she sprinted to catch up.

"Luke! Hey, Luke! Wait up.''

He stopped and turned, and when she caught up to him, Morgan felt herself blushing.

It was his fault. He seemed to be staring at her mouth, and that dratted kiss was right there between them, just as she'd feared it would be. She swallowed hard and forced herself to look straight into his eyes, struggling for a professional tone. "I'd like to speak to you privately for a moment,'' she managed to croak.

"Of course. Come in here." He opened the

door of an unoccupied examining room, holding it until she was inside.

She'd never realized how small these rooms really were, Morgan thought as she squeezed past him, too aware of his warmth, his particular male essence. There was a single plastic chair and the examining table, with a bare two feet of open space between them, and her foot caught the chair and sent it toppling.

"Ooops—"

"Got it—"

She lunged for it and so did he. Their shoulders collided and both of them pulled back. Luke lifted the chair with one hand and set it upright. He seemed enormous in the confined space.

"Morgan, I—"

"Luke, I wanted—"

They both stopped, and she returned his polite smile, though her lips felt numb.

He made a tiny bow and a courtly little gesture with his hand, inviting her to begin again, and then he leaned back against the examining table, one hand in the pocket of his dark slacks, his entire attention focused on her.

His long body was nonchalant and graceful as he waited for her to speak.

Admit it Morgan. He's drop-dead handsome, and sexy, too. Every cell in her body acknowledged it.

Her throat was dry, and she was trembling a little, of all the silly things. She sank down on the chair and realized right away that it was a mistake, because now her eyes were in a direct line with his crotch.

Lordy. She tipped her head back and stared up at his face with dogged determination.

"Luke, I wanted to thank you for coming to the funeral—it was kind and thoughtful of you. I also wanted to tell you I was talking to Frannie Myles this afternoon."

Morgan found herself speaking faster than normal. She tried to slow down as she explained about the group Frannie was starting, adding, "I just thought I'd mention it to you in case you thought it was a good thing for Sophie. I hope Tessa's going to go."

He nodded. He was looking at her intently, and as usual, it was impossible to read his expression, which made her even more nervous. She wondered if she ought to have said anything at all. After all, hadn't he told her how he felt about someone from the hospital counseling Sophie? Maybe he thought she was meddling.

She grew more and more uncomfortable when he remained silent for several more moments. He just looked at her steadily, and she started to get the awful feeling that he regretted having ever mentioned his daughter to her. She could feel herself flushing all over again, and she first cursed her coloring, then, in self-defense, she cursed him for making her feel so darned uneasy.

Just when she'd decided to either get to her feet and walk out or say something rude just to break the tension, he cleared his throat and said, "Morgan, would you care to have dinner with me?"

"*Dinner?*"

Astounded, she repeated the word as if she'd never heard it before.

"Dinner. You know, where people sit in a decent restaurant and a waiter brings platters of food and drink?"

"Dinner. Yeah, now I remember. Umm, sure, I guess so. When?" Darn. She couldn't seem to manage more than idiotic phrases.

"What's today, Tuesday? How about Friday? I'm on call, but as far as I know none of my patients is due to deliver. What about yours?"

She could barely remember that she even had patients, she felt so absolutely stunned by this turn of events. Finally she shrugged and shook her head. "I don't think anybody's due."

"Good. So you're free Friday?"

She nodded like a marionette.

"Then I'll pick you up at your house, say, at seven?"

"Seven. Friday." She was doing it again, acting like a zombie. She had to get out of this room while she still had some semblance of a brain. She got to her feet, and he straightened and opened the door for her.

She walked past him, helplessly breathing in the scent of him, every pore aware of his nearness. She nodded and gave him a small, strained smile and then hurried off down the corridor feeling as if she'd been hit by a truck.

"YOU'RE GOING OUT for dinner with Doc Gilbert?" For the first time since her baby's death, Tessa showed a trace of her old animation that evening when Morgan blurted out her news. "So what're ya gonna wear?"

Morgan shrugged. "I've been thinking maybe I ought to call and cancel. He caught me sort of off guard, and I said yes before I really thought it through." She'd been in a kind of daze all afternoon, and now she was having serious second thoughts about the whole thing. "It's been a couple of years since I've gone out on anything remotely like a date," she confessed. "And now that I think about it, it wasn't my finest hour even then."

In fact, most of her experiences along that line had been nothing short of calamitous. She just wasn't good at making small talk or playing the games that dating seemed to require.

"Besides, we work together. It's a really bad idea to date somebody you work with." She'd heard the nurses at the hospital talking about that very thing, and everybody seemed to agree that it was a big mistake.

"Oh, phooey." Tessa blew a raspberry and waved a dismissive hand. "That's only if you're dating the boss. Doc Gilbert's not your boss—you're sort of equals, aren't you?"

Morgan bristled. "Absolutely, we're equals. In fact, technically, I'm the senior obstetrician at the clinic."

"So? There ya go. He's kinda cute for an old guy, so why not go for it? If dinner's a flop, just take along money for a taxi home."

Morgan grinned, delighted that Tess was making jokes again. She was repeating exactly what Morgan had always told her: if you ran into a situation that made you uncomfortable, make sure you had money for a taxi.

If only she'd taken a cab home on that last date with Dylan.

Tessa was giving Morgan a speculative once-over. "You really oughta get your hair cut—it could use a trim. I hear there's a hot new hairdresser at Shapers. Why not give him a try?"

Morgan whipped her head from side to side,

but Tessa wasn't dissuaded. "Look, that place you usually go to is the pits, Morgan, face it. They're all way too old to know what's hot. Besides, there's this boutique right across the street from Shapers. Maybe we could, like, find you a dress or something?" Her voice took on more of the animation it had lost. "You know, you oughta do something about your work clothes while we're at it. Those cord pants and sweaters you wear all the time gotta go. C'mon, Morgan, let's go shopping and get you up to speed."

Haircuts always made Morgan nervous, even at the salon she'd been going to for years. And buying clothes was her least favorite activity. But it was wonderful to have Tessa taking an interest in something again. This was the first enthusiasm she'd shown for anything since the baby's funeral, and Morgan felt it was worth a sacrifice on her part if it would help Tessa.

"Well, I guess. Maybe. But nothing too drastic, promise?"

Tess rolled her eyes. "Man, you sound like you're havin' a root canal." She picked up the phone and called for a hair appointment at Shapers.

"The mall's not far from the hair place, we can go there for shoes," she decided, and Morgan felt her heart sink. Hair, clothes, shoes. She groaned. It was going to be a long, painful afternoon.

LUKE MADE HIS WAY up her front stairs at precisely three minutes before seven that Friday evening, holding the bouquet of sunflowers he'd finally tracked down. The golden retriever he'd met on his last visit was lying on a mat outside the front door, and the dog rose to his feet and barked, pretending to be ferocious.

"Major, you old phony. Remember me?" Luke bent down and rubbed behind the dog's floppy ears, and Major leaned against him, his tail smacking Luke's pant leg in ecstasy.

Luke gave the dog one last pat and knocked on the door, wondering how in bloody hell he'd gotten himself into this.

He'd had serious misgivings ever since the invitation sprang from his mouth without consulting his brain, and right at this moment, he wished with all his being that one of his soon-to-be moms had chosen tonight to begin labor.

"Hi, Doc. Morgan's nearly ready. Come on in." Tessa was far too thin, Luke thought as he greeted the girl and stepped inside the house.

"Those for Morgan?" Tessa's big hazel eyes dwarfed her face. The left eye still had green-and-yellow bruises surrounding it, and there were dark circles beneath both. Her spiky hair showed dark brown roots beneath the mottled purple and yellow.

"Yes. Perhaps you could put them somewhere?" He felt ridiculous holding them. "And these are for you." He dug the small box of hand-dipped chocolates from his jacket.

"Wow, thanks! How'd ya know I'm a chocoholic?" She looked genuinely pleased. "Thank you for the flowers you sent for Ky—" Her voice broke and she swallowed hard. "For Kyla's funeral, too," she managed to add. "It was very thoughtful of you."

The formal little speech touched his heart, and Luke reached out and took her bony shoulder in his hand, giving it a reassuring squeeze. "I only wish there'd been something more I could have done," he said, his voice thick with emotion.

He still couldn't look at Tessa without thinking of Sophie, and he wished again he hadn't made this date. His daughter was home, sulking in her room.

"You brought me sunflowers, Luke? How'd you do that at this time of year?" Morgan asked from the stairwell.

He turned, suddenly as nervous as a teenager, and then he simply gaped at the sight of her. She was standing on the staircase, two steps up, and the unruly mass of tousled hair was now a short, curly cap that outlined the contours of her well-

shaped head, baring pixieish ears and accentu-
ating her slender, graceful neck. A few long,
wispy bangs hung over her forehead, making her
chocolate brown eyes immense and luminous.

She was wearing something short, gently
shaped and black. A dress with a V neckline that
skimmed rather than outlined her body. It em-
phasized full breasts and stopped well short of
her knees, showing off silk-sheathed legs. Her
high heels had sexy little straps that crossed on
her instep, and she carried a short jacket that
matched her dress.

By God, she was beautiful. He stared at her,
drinking her in with his eyes, finally regaining
his composure and his voice.

"Morgan. Morgan, you look stunning."

She blushed a rosy pink, and he realized that
he'd been anticipating that telltale flush. To him,
it had become Morgan's trademark, and he'd
sometimes instigated it by provoking her to either pleasure or anger.

"Tessa redid me, top to toe. Even the makeup," she said with touching ingenuousness, the
slight tremor in her deep voice revealing her ner-
vousness. "Truth is, I don't really feel like me
at all." She took the last two steps down and
then stumbled, making an undignified lunge for
the banister an instant before Luke grabbed her
bare arm.

She regained her balance and looked up at him, rolling her eyes and twisting her face into a rueful grimace. "*Now* I feel like me. You can dress me up, but you can't take me out. I never really learned to walk properly in heels."

Luke laughed and then realized he'd held her arm several heartbeats too long. He let go and stepped back, and from behind him Tessa smothered a giggle.

It did Luke's heart good to hear it, and he winked at Morgan. "I'm sure you'll do fine with those shoes. You just need a little more practice," he teased, taking the jacket from her and helping her into it, allowing his hands to brush against the soft skin of her arms.

"Don't be too late," Tessa deadpanned as they walked out the door. "You've got work in the morning, Morgan."

"Brat." Morgan turned around and stuck her tongue out at the girl, and Luke noted that Tessa was still smiling as she closed the door behind them.

"Let's use an ounce of prevention here. I don't fancy setting a broken bone just now." Luke used the heels as an excuse to slip an arm around Morgan's waist as they descended the porch steps, pretending to steady her but actually enjoying the narrowness of her waist and the swell of her hips under his hand. She smelled delicious—some light and haunting fragrance that pleased him.

In fact, everything about her pleased him, he realized as he opened the car door and helped her inside. He heard the sensual rustle of her hosiery as she slid across the leather seat, and a jolt of pure animal hunger shot through him.

He wanted this woman. He wanted her in his arms, in his bed. It was simply sex, he assured himself as he spoke to her about the unexpected sunshine Vancouver was enjoying and the unlikely chance that maybe the weather would last through the weekend.

It was pure body hunger, this attraction he felt, some unlikely match of pheromones or something.

Although he hadn't actually dated anyone since Deborah's death, for the past two years he hadn't been celibate, either. There'd been casual encounters with several women who'd wanted exactly what he had to give, sex without strings, without real intimacy, without anything more than simple appeasement of human need.

Was that going to be possible with Morgan? She was the first specific woman he'd wanted for a long time, and he found that fact upsetting. Somehow he'd have to make it clear to her that he wasn't looking for a lasting relationship.

He slid the car into gear and pulled onto the

street, touching the button on the dash that would activate the tape in the stereo.

"Fats Domino? You actually like rock and roll?" She sounded astonished.

"I can change it if you prefer."

"Nope, I love him. I figured you'd be more the classical type."

He turned to her, raised an eyebrow and assumed an injured air. "Just because I have an accent, you've pegged me as a snob? Show a bit of humility here, Dr. Jacobsen. You can be wrong, you know."

She stared at him for a moment. "Man, you got that right," she said with feeling, and then she laughed, the deep, hearty belly laugh that made his insides feel warm.

For no real reason, he laughed with her. It had been a long time since he'd done so with genuine amusement, and all of a sudden he knew it was going to be a good evening.

"So, WHERE DID YOU do your internship?" Seated across from Luke in the cozy little restaurant he'd chosen, Morgan began to relax. The tables were far enough apart, the lighting was soft, the music pleasant but muted. There were just enough empty tables to lend a sense of privacy.

The noise level was low and the service excellent. Most amazing of all, for the first time in her entire adult life, Morgan felt well dressed and actually quite attractive.

Well, passable. And she hadn't spilled a single thing, at least not yet.

"At St. Bart's. It's near St. Paul's Cathedral in London's East End. After that I did another year at an obstetrical clinic much like Women's Place. It was a great opportunity for an obstetrician—our case load was enormous. What about you?"

"Oh, St. Joe's, of course. Where else?"

He nodded. "I should have guessed. I've noticed that you're on a first-name basis with everyone from the housekeeping staff to the administrator."

"Well, not quite the administrator." She sipped the wine and added, "He's new. I can't really say I know him very well. It takes time."

He gave her a wry grin. "I think I told you before you have a magical way with people."

She felt her cheeks flush with pleasure. "Thank you. I guess it makes up for having two left feet."

"What makes you think that?"

She wrinkled her nose at him. "C'mon. Stop being polite, Luke." This lovely wine was going to her head, just a little. "Surely you must have noticed that things have a way of getting a bit

muddled when I'm around? When I was interning, my nickname was Flap Jacobsen. Residents
shuddered and took tranquilizers when I rotated
to their service. I had trouble with strict routines,
and I used to lose stuff a lot.''

He looked puzzled. ''What kind of things did
you lose?''

''Oh, instruments, charts, orders. A cadaver
once or twice, but that wasn't my fault. The guys
in the morgue kept playing jokes on me. Although a couple of times patients got misplaced
for an hour or two. You know, the surgical rotation was the very worst. Those guys are so anal
about the tiniest things, like clamps and sterile
procedure and stuff.'' She held her hands up in
a ''Go figure'' gesture.

He laughed, and she thought how much laughter suited him. His dark-lashed eyes crinkled,
and attractive lines appeared beside his mouth.
He had strong, straight teeth.

He didn't laugh enough, she decided. But of
course, what with his wife's death and now his
daughter's pregnancy, he probably didn't have a
whole lot to laugh about.

''That's what was so great about obstetrics,''
she went on with unfeigned enthusiasm. ''I'm
right at home. Babies come when they feel like
it. In the delivery room a flap is the norm instead
of the exception. And the birth process.'' She

widened her eyes and shook her head. "Gosh, it's the biggest miracle. There's never any possibility of getting bored."

He saw the glow in her eyes, the passion for the job she loved, and he nodded agreement. "As long as things go well, it's the very best specialty there is. When they go bad, it tears your heart out." A shadow crossed his face, and Morgan knew he was thinking of Tessa's baby, just as she was. He was probably also thinking of Sophie and her pregnancy.

She wondered if he'd given any thought to the group Frannie was forming. She wondered, too, if she had the right to ask more about Sophie. Surely they ought to be open and honest with each other if this newfound friendship was going to work? She threw caution to the winds.

"Speaking of babies, how's your daughter doing, Luke?"

His face was suffused with pain for an instant. "Physically, well enough. She's still furious with me, so there's not a lot of communication between us."

"What's she so mad about?"

"Everything I say or do, it seems."

"Gosh, I'm sorry. That's so tough on both of you. Is there someone she's close to, somebody she can talk with?"

He considered the question and then shook his

head. "I have a housekeeper, but Sophie and Eileen don't get on."

"Then maybe you ought to get another one, someone she likes better." Morgan realized her comment wasn't particularly polite. She was too accustomed to saying exactly what was on her mind, she chided herself.

He looked at her for a long moment, his expression unreadable, and she was afraid he was going to tell her to mind her own business. But then he gave a reluctant nod.

"I've thought of doing that, but we've had a series of housekeepers since my wife's death, and Sophie's reacted the same way to all of them. She resents everyone I hire."

"Why not let her do the hiring?"

He shot her a scandalized look. It was obvious the thought had never crossed his mind.

"Probably losing her mother was pretty traumatic for her," Morgan went on recklessly. "Kids sometimes react with anger when actually they're feeling sorrow. I didn't know that myself, but Frannie pointed it out. Not just kids, either. Weren't you angry when your wife died, Luke?"

Too late, she realized that she'd overstepped some boundary, because Luke's jaw had tightened ominously and a muscle jumped beside his mouth.

His green eyes had gone cold and still.

CHAPTER NINE

MORGAN FELT acutely uncomfortable.

Luke obviously didn't want to talk about his daughter or his wife's death, but there was one more thing she wanted to mention.

"Tessa's going to join that group I told you about. The first meeting's next Monday night."

"Yes, I heard. I took your advice and spoke to Frannie Myles yesterday," he surprised her by saying. "I told Sophie about the meeting. It sounds like something she needs."

"D'you think she'll go?"

Luke shook his head. "I have no idea."

The waiter came to clear the dinner plates and ask about dessert and coffee, and when he left, Luke changed the subject. "Did you grow up in Vancouver, Morgan?"

It was obvious he wanted them back on neutral ground. She shook her head in answer to his question, wondering how much of her life she ought to reveal. Undoubtedly, her childhood had been the complete opposite of his.

"I was born in Los Angeles, and I lived there

until I finished high school. My mother was a Hollywood actress.''

He raised his brows in surprise. "Would I have seen her work in the cinema?"

"Maybe. Not too likely. India tried both stage and screen, but she never made it big. She did quite a few commercials, though, and she had a few small parts in some dusters. Her name's actually Gertrude. She'd murder me if she knew I told anyone.''

He looked interested, so Morgan went on, "She's retired now. She's sixty-four and living in a trailer in Florida. I go down to see her every couple of years."

Less, actually. It had been three and a half years since the last awkward visit. "We're not very close—we never were.''

The subject of her mother wasn't an easy one. Memories of growing up with India were still excruciatingly painful; Morgan usually hid that pain behind a facade of humor, turning her lonely, chaotic childhood into a cartoon sketch. She didn't feel like doing that now. "How about you, Luke? Did you have a mom who wore an apron and baked cookies?''

The very idea of his mother making cookies must have been preposterous, because it made him tilt his head back and laugh. "My mother knows nothing about cooking. We always had help to do that sort of thing."

Morgan stopped eating and leaned toward him. "Servants? You mean you actually had servants?"

He shrugged. "Well, people who performed the necessary household tasks, certainly. But that was when I was a child and the family still had money. My father died seven years ago. Mother sold most of the estate and lives quite simply now."

"It sounds as if you grew up in one of those English mansions." She could see him in that setting. "Did you?"

"I did, and I can tell you, they're cold as hell. I very much appreciate central heating."

"So you went to private schools and all that?" The awe in her voice brought a whimsical smile to his lips.

"In England we call them public schools, just to be contrary. I was shipped off at the age of five. It's not the perfect way to spend a childhood, believe me. But then, I doubt there are many perfect childhoods."

Morgan doubted it, too, although she was pretty sure most had to be better than the one she'd had. "Were you an only child, too?"

He nodded. "Mother had had another baby many years before I was born, but he died at the age of three. My parents were already quite old when I came along. Mother was forty-two and Father was fifty, and they obviously hadn't planned on having me. Their lives were busy and regulated—golfing, hunting, fishing in Scotland, that sort of thing. I was a nuisance.''

Morgan nodded, even though the life he described was only familiar from the movies. But she suspected there was at least one same element in his childhood that had been in hers—loneliness.

"Like you, Morgan, I'm not particularly close to my mother. We exchange letters every several months."

"She's never come to Canada for a visit?"

"Oh, yes, twice. Once when I was married and again when my wife was killed. It was fairly strained both times."

"And have you gone back to England?"

"Once. For a medical conference a year before my father died. I took Deborah and Sophie." He grimaced. "It wasn't exactly a successful visit. Sophie developed measles and my mother was terrified everyone in the house would get them, most of all herself. She's very concerned with her health."

"My mother's obsessed with her appearance," Morgan said. "India's beautiful, and I was a big disappointment to her. I think she's always believed that the hospital made a mistake, because as a kid I looked sort of like J. Edgar Hoover with carroty hair.''

He didn't smile. Instead his eyes traveled over her face like a caress, and he said, ''You've certainly changed since then.''

''C'mon, Luke. Don't tease.'' Totally flustered by the compliment and at a loss for something to say, Morgan took a big bite of the chocolate cheesecake she'd ordered.

''Mmm, you ought to try some of this. Here—have a spoonful.'' She held it out to him. Instead of taking the spoon from her, he opened his mouth and allowed her to feed him. His lips closed, slowly, sensually, intimately, around the spoon, and his eyes met hers and seemed to smolder with banked desire. A wave of pure longing rolled over her. It made her nervous, and she felt immense relief when he continued their conversation.

''You haven't mentioned your father, Morgan.''

''That's because I never really met him. India was a marrying fool. It was the only thing she and Liz Taylor had in common. I had five stepfathers, as well as my own real father, of course. He was India's first husband and he left when I was a couple of months old, never to be heard from again. I think my mother's been married six times in all, but I may have lost count.''

"And were they kind to you, all those stepfathers?"

Morgan gave him a candid look. "None of them molested me, which I now realize was just plain luck. Mostly they ignored me. Some I didn't really know very well, and I doubt India did, either. They weren't even around long enough for me to get their names straight."

Her voice softened. "There was one special guy, though. I used to pretend he was my real father—husband number five. Pete Mahoney, a builder. Actually, it was because of Pete that I ended up in medicine."

"He encouraged you?"

"Nope. Oh, he probably would have if we'd ever talked about it, but we didn't. I never in my wildest dreams thought of being a doctor back then. I just wanted to get through high school and move far away from India because we weren't getting along. Pete married her when I was fourteen. He lasted three years and five months, which was some kind of record, and he and I became good friends. Pete was a thoroughly nice guy, the closest I ever got to having a real father. And he stayed my friend even though India divorced him and went on to marry someone else."

She frowned, trying to recall who came next in India's marriage roster. "Jackson, was it? Or maybe it was Theo. I can't remember. Anyhow, all during high school Pete would call and take me out for a burger and we'd sit and talk, he'd listen to all my far-fetched ideas and make sure I had enough spending money. He came to my high school graduation. When I moved here we wrote, and in one of the last letters I got, he said he wasn't feeling well. I wanted to go see him, but I had the café at that time and it was next to impossible to get away, so I kept putting it off."

She stared down at her dessert plate, remembering.

"You had a café?" Luke's deep voice encouraged her to go on with her story. She glanced up to find he was giving her all his attention, forgetting even to drink his coffee, and she was both embarrassed and flattered.

She hadn't planned to monopolize the entire conversation with stories about her past. "Yeah, you know the Firehouse Grill over on Fourth? Well, I started that. It's a lot fancier now than when I had it. It was just a little hole-in-the-wall place I rented for next to nothing, but the food was pretty good."

She tilted her chin up. "Actually, I'm a great short-order cook. I just don't get much time to do it anymore. Anyhow, I didn't go to see Pete, and next thing I heard he'd died.'' She was quiet for a moment, reliving the guilt and awful grief she'd suffered at that time. ''He left me a substantial inheritance,'' she added in a quiet tone. ''Enough to pay my way through medical school.''

She looked up, straight into Luke's thoughtful eyes, and gave him a rueful smile. ''Pete worked hard all his life, and I figured I ought to do something worthwhile with his money, so I sold the grill and started university. One thing led to another, and I ended up in medicine.''

She sat back in her chair, drew in a deep breath and let it out again. How had she ended up telling him all this stuff?

''So, now you know all about my checkered past. I'm a real bore when I get going. Sorry.''

''No, you're not. Nobody can ever accuse you of being boring, my dear.'' The steady look he gave her sent a wave of heat coursing through her body. His voice was rough edged, and it seemed to caress her like a touch. ''I think I've told you before that I find you a lovely and quite fascinating woman.''

She finally remembered what to do with a compliment.

''Thank you,'' she said, and then grinned at him and crossed her eyes. But the words and the way he said them stayed with her for the rest of the magical evening.

They lingered over coffee, discussed seeing a show or going to a club, but instead, they strolled down Vancouver's nighttime streets like tourists, looking in shop windows, watching the passing parade, not even talking very much.

At some point, Luke took her hand in his, and Morgan was astounded at the sensations that assailed her. She'd never considered herself a particularly sensual woman. Certainly, as far as she knew, men had never been attracted to her in a passionate way. There'd been one short-lived sexual encounter at university, and another, more intense and longer lasting, when she was interning. She'd fallen in love that second time, deeply and romantically. As it turned out, Glen had, too...with someone else.

That breakup had been incredibly painful. Unlike India, who seemed content with quantity instead of quality, Morgan had always dreamed of creating the stable family unit she'd never had as a child, the adoring husband she'd grow old with, the half-dozen babies of her own. Happily ever after.

She'd thought her heart was literally breaking when Glen left, and for a long time she avoided involvement. That was when she'd decided on obstetrics. If she wasn't having her own babies, she'd deliver other people's.

Even though it was difficult at first, she'd stayed friends with Glen, and she'd pretended to be happy when he'd gone on to marry the other woman. She'd attended his wedding and even ended up delivering two of his babies.

By then, she was totally over him, thank goodness, and she *was* happy again. Obstetrics was both demanding and time-consuming and marvelous. Her late twenties passed in a blur of work, and by her early thirties, she realized she'd mastered the knack of turning would-be suitors into buddies. Maybe she was never intended to be a wife and mother, she rationalized. She'd bought her house, and then Tessa came along, and now she had a family of sorts.

And then came Luke.

She'd never experienced anything like the powerful sexual reaction she felt now, just having his fingers threaded through hers. He absently stroked his thumb over her knuckles, and once he lifted her hand and pressed his lips to it.

At last they made their way back to the lot where the car was parked.

"I guess I should get home," she said with reluctance. "Saturday office hours." It was her turn.

"It's not that late. What about a drive?"

"Okay," she agreed before the words were fully out of his mouth, and they both laughed.

Like teenagers reluctant to end a date, they agreed on a slow circuit of Stanley Park; they discovered that neither of them had taken the time to do that for years.

It was a clear, calm night, and the lights from the houses on the North Shore mountains reflected in the waters of the inlet. Luke pulled the car into one of the viewpoints and turned off the motor and the lights.

Morgan's heart began to hammer. In the darkness, she could see only his profile, the chiseled perfection of forehead, his strong nose, his powerful jaw. He turned slightly, reaching across the gearshift mechanism and capturing her hand once again.

His crisp British baritone was soft, even a bit hesitant. "I've enjoyed this evening more than I can say, Morgan. It's been good getting to know you." He paused, a note of sad irony in his tone when he continued. "There aren't really many people I confide in. The man I considered my closest friend is the father of the boy responsible for Sophie's pregnancy." His voice hardened. "Needless to say, we're not friends any longer."

Morgan gave his fingers a sympathetic squeeze. "I understand, because I sure don't feel friendly toward Dylan Volger, either. After the baby's funeral, I confronted him. It was all I could do not to physically attack him, I was so mad."

He made a small sound in his throat. "I must confess, I came close to smashing my fist into Jason's nose at one point. I never realized I could lose control that quickly or completely." He fell silent, and then after what seemed a long time, his voice deepened, and he added, "The only other time I felt that total loss of control was when I kissed you the other day, Morgan."

She knew all of a sudden that he was planning to kiss her again, and she panicked. The intimacy of the car's interior, the charged emotion that was suddenly between them made her breath catch in her throat. "Let's get out for a minute, okay?" Without waiting for his answer, she fumbled the car door open.

The night was soft and very dark, and she fled recklessly down a flight of stone steps, heading for a small observation terrace where a single streetlight burned.

She was terribly aware of him when he caught up with her halfway toward her destination. He slid his arm around her shoulders, steadying her when she stumbled in her unfamiliar shoes. She moved straight toward the light, pausing only when she was directly beneath it.

Luke took her shoulders in each of his hands. "Talk to me, Morgan." There was a thread of anger in his voice. "Why the hell does the thought of my kissing you upset you so?"

"Because." She could hardly get her breath. "Because we have to work together, and because...because passion turns people into total maniacs. I've watched it disrupt whole teams at St. Joe's. We're far too busy to complicate everything that way, and I'd...I'd rather just be your friend—" *you liar, Morgan* "—and because... Oh, darn," she wailed. "Because I'm scared. I'm just not much good at, umm, at all this stuff."

His laugh was a low rumble, and his arms came around her and drew her hard against him. "Why not let me be the judge of that?" he murmured an instant before his lips came down on hers.

Morgan felt the instant sweet pleasure of arousal as his arms drew her closer, so that her breasts pressed against him and her hips touched his thighs. He kissed her gently, an inquiring kiss, until at last she opened her mouth, allowing him to explore with his tongue, and the deepening intimacy sent a quiver of longing through her.

Heat pooled in her abdomen, and she forgot about caution. She stood on tiptoe and looped her arms around his neck, pressing herself even closer against the male hardness of his body.

She was at a disadvantage, because she was so much shorter than he, but an impatient groan rose from his throat and he lifted her feet off the ground, angling their bodies so that she was achingly aware of his erection and helpless in his embrace.

She'd been celibate for so long. Every suppressed impulse rose to the surface, and she drank in his kisses like nectar, undulating her hips against him.

The sound of a car door slamming penetrated the delicious fog of pleasure that surrounded them, and Luke set her on her feet, his arm protectively around her.

A patrol car had pulled up beside Luke's vehicle.

"Evenin', folks." A uniformed policeman trotted down the stairs and moved into the pool of light where they stood under the streetlamp. He was young, and he gave them a knowing but apologetic grin. "Sorry to interrupt, but your car's sitting up there with the keys in it and the doors are unlocked. We've had problems with car theft in this area, so it's best not to extend an open invitation like that."

"Thanks, Officer." Luke's voice was ragged and he cleared his throat. "We'll be on our way." The policeman hurried back up the stairs, whistling as he went, and climbed into his car.

Luke grasped Morgan's hand and led the way up the stairs. Back in the car, he didn't start the motor at once. Instead, he expelled a long, shaky breath and lifted her fingers to his lips, caressing each of her chapped knuckles with his mouth.

"I want you in my bed, Morgan. I intend to have you there unless you have better objections than the ones you raised a while ago."

She tried to remember what they'd been, but for the life of her, she couldn't recall. The only thing she knew with any certainty was that she wanted exactly what he wanted, the sooner the better. But imagining being in bed with Luke caused her practical mind to immediately come up with a whole new set of problems.

"I don't see how we can manage that," she blurted. "We can't very well go to my house— Tessa's there. And you've got Sophie, as well as your housekeeper, at yours. And going to a motel isn't something I care to do."

He gave her a dumbfounded look that made her realize he hadn't considered the actual mechanics of the thing at all, and then he rhymed off a string of obscenities. Morgan found it impressive that foul language could sound so cultured.

"You're right. Bloody hell! Well, leave it

with me—I'll come up with something." He turned on the ignition and the car roared to life, and in the midst of her disappointment Morgan told herself that having nowhere to go to make love right this moment might be a good thing.

Their lives were complicated enough already, and going to bed together wasn't going to make things any easier for either of them. This delay would give them both time to cool off and figure out whether or not being together was a good idea, she told herself, trying to be adult and reasonable and patient.

Reasonable, patient, phooey! Morgan leaned her head against the leather seat and blinked hard. She felt a lot like crying.

Wouldn't you know just when she was ready to throw caution to the winds and leap into bed with a drop-dead handsome man, there wasn't a bed available?

CHAPTER TEN

THE FIRST MEETING of Connections, the support group for teenagers dealing with issues centered around pregnancy and parenting, ended at eight-fifteen on Monday evening, and Sophie was the first to bolt out of the stuffy room. She hurried down the hallway of the community center, heading for fresh air and freedom.

"Sophie! Hey, Sophie Gilbert. Wait up."

Surprised and wary, Sophie paused as one of the girls from the group trotted up the hall and stopped beside her.

There'd been seven females trapped back there for an hour and a half, three like Sophie, pregnant but not showing too much yet, one who looked about to pop, an older girl who'd given her baby up for adoption and wanted it back. And there was that social-work type, of course. Frannie What's-Her-Name, who'd organized this whole dumb thing and kept asking questions like "How do you feel about that?" and "Do you care to share your experiences with the others?"

It was depressing and totally gross, Sophie decided. And then there was this girl with her purple hair and the rings in her nose and ears. Tessa something or other.

"Hey," the girl continued, "your dad's Doc Gilbert, right? I know him—he works with my foster mom, Morgan Jacobsen. My name's Tessa Hargraves in case you didn't catch it in the meeting."

Sophie gave her another sidelong glance, wondering what this bone rack of a girl with her fluorescent spiky hair and black leather biker jacket wanted with her. She'd told them at the meeting that she'd had a baby a month ago, but it died.

Sophie had pretty much managed to block the others out, but she'd felt sorry about Tessa's baby, because she knew all about death, how awful it hurt inside when someone you loved died. "Yeah, I remember you. I'm real sorry about your baby," she muttered now.

"Yeah, thanks." Tessa's voice lost its vivacity.

"My mother died," Sophie blurted out. "Four years ago. In a car accident." She hadn't planned to say that. The words had just popped out for some reason.

"Oh, yeah? I never had a real mom," Tessa volunteered. "At least not one I remember, but it must be hard, having one and then losing her like that. Were you, like, close to her?''

"Yeah. Real close. We used to do stuff together, shopping and manicures and stuff.'' Sophie's throat closed and she gulped, blinking back tears. This was too weird, having somebody she barely knew talk to her like this. The kids in Victoria whom she'd considered her best friends had avoided her after her mom died. It was as if death were like AIDS or something they were scared to catch. When her father'd moved them to Vancouver and she changed schools, she'd been real careful not to bring up anything about her mother dying. The only people she'd talked about it with were Jason and his family.

"Having somebody die on you really sucks,'' she added with vehemence.

Tessa nodded, her face somber. "Yeah. It's like it leaves an empty hole inside ya.'' They were standing outside now. It was wet and rainy, and Tessa shivered. "It's freezin' out here. You wanna hot chocolate or something, Sophie? There's a fast-food place just a coupla blocks away.''

"Yeah, that sounds good.'' Sophie hadn't really hung out with anybody since her breakup with Jason. Her best girlfriend, Tiffany, had dropped Sophie fast when she'd confided that

she was pregnant. Pregnancy and death had a lot
in common, Sophie figured. People didn't know
what to say or how to act in either situation.

They exchanged information as they hurried
along the sidewalk—about the special classes for
pregnant teens, the teachers they loved or hated.
Inside the restaurant, they ordered and slid into
a booth.

"So, when's your baby coming?" Tessa
found a tiny mirror in her shoulder bag and carefully checked her makeup, using a tissue to wipe
away mascara that had smeared.

"March twenty-third." Sophie watched as the
other girl extracted a purple lip pencil from her
bag and applied it to her full mouth.

"Is it movin' around yet?"

Sophie shrugged. "I dunno. How do you
tell?"

"Oh, you'll know when it starts. At first it's
sorta, like, these little butterfly wings, and then
after a while you can feel feet just bootin' you
from the inside."

Tessa's eyes suddenly filled with tears and
overflowed, and she dabbed at them with the
sleeve of her shirt, trying not to smear her mascara again. "Shit. Sorry, it's just that I get
thinkin' about Kyla. She shoulda only been gettin' born next month. I wake up in the morning

sometimes and for a minute I think she's still inside me."

She scrabbled in her handbag and pulled out a package of cigarettes. "I was off these things when I was pregnant. I gotta try to quit again." Her hand shook as she took one out and lit it.

Sophie saw how much Tessa was hurting and she wanted to help, but she wasn't sure how. She only knew for sure that it was better to talk about the person who'd died than ignore the grief. "That was her name, Kyla? That's so pretty. I really like that. I haven't thought of names yet." The truth was, she hadn't really thought of the baby much at all, not as a live human being with a face and a name. The anger and sense of injustice she'd fortified herself with for so long slipped a little, and fear crept up her spine.

"D'you mind if I ask you some stuff, Tessa? About, umm, having babies and that kinda thing?" She'd wanted to ask in the meeting tonight, but she'd felt like such a dork.

"Nope. Go ahead."

"Does it, like, really *hurt* when...it gets born?"

Tessa looked her straight in the eye and nodded. "Yeah, it does. At least, it did for me."

Her face tightened and her hazel eyes took on a faraway look. "But I had an accident, see, and it was all happenin' too soon and real fast, so they couldn't give me anything, right? Morgan says usually they do this thing called an epidural if it's hurtin' real bad, and that makes it easier. But I couldn't have one.''

Sophie thought that over for a few minutes, and they sipped their chocolate in silence. ''So you can talk to Morgan, huh? Ask her questions and stuff?''

Tessa raised her plucked eyebrows and spread her hands. ''Hey, like of *course* I can talk to her. She's my friend, right? I mean, she's my foster mom, technically, but she's a baby doctor, so she knows all the right answers.'' Tessa tipped her head to the side and gave Sophie a curious look. ''But so's your dad, right? He helped when Kyla...''

Sophie nodded, lowering her head so her hair partly obscured her face. ''Yeah. But I wouldn't ask *him* anything.'' Her voice dripped with disdain.

''So, like, he's totally freaked about you being pregnant, right?''

Sophie's head shot up and she glared at Tessa. ''Did this Morgan tell you that?'' Was her father discussing her with everyone? If so, it was one more betrayal to add to the list, and the ache in her chest that had eased a little during the past half hour came back again with a vengeance.

''Hey, don't go ballistic on me. I guessed by

the way your voice goes when you talk about him."

"Oh. Yeah. Sorry." Embarrassed, Sophie let her shoulders slump and she toyed with her empty cup, tearing off pieces of foam and crumpling them.

"So, what's the score with the genetic donor? He on the scene or did he split?"

"The...the who?" Sophie was still thinking of her father.

"You know, the boyfriend. Your main squeeze. The kid's father."

"Oh. Jason." It even to hurt say his name. "When my dad found out about the baby, he had this *huge* fight with Jason and his dad, and I haven't seen Jason since." Sophie glanced at Tessa. "How about you?"

"His name's Dylan." Tessa shook her head and avoided Sophie's gaze, tapping her cigarette into an ashtray. "Things didn't work out, so I broke up with him." She took a long drink of her chocolate.

"You still miss him?" Sophie cried every single night, longing for Jason.

Tessa shrugged. "I'm, like, real pissed off at him, but I miss him, too, ya know?" She shot a hopeless glance at Sophie and shrugged expressively. "Go figure, huh?"

"Yeah. It's the same with me." The hurt

she'd never admitted even to herself spilled out now. "He could call me—it's not as if there're telephone police—or meet me somewhere." It was such a relief, being able to share a little of how she really felt with somebody who understood.

"Guys freak when you get knocked up, I guess." Tessa glanced at her watch. "Yikes. I've gotta go. I told Morgan I'd walk the dogs for her 'cause she's on call tonight." She stood up and grabbed her leather jacket, shoving her arms into the sleeves.

"You've got dogs?" Sophie was envious.

"Yeah, two. Skippy and Major. And a kitten called Flower. Morgan can't resist strays, so we agreed she's not allowed to go near the pound anymore. She picks the ones nobody else'll take, Skippy's deaf and sorta neurotic—he's kinda my dog. Major's older and crippled, and the cat's only got one eye."

"I wish we had a dog. We couldn't because my mom was allergic."

"Well, you'll just hafta c'mon over and meet ours." Tessa hesitated, suddenly shy. "Hey, I'm learning to cook. You wanna come for supper one night this week? How about tomorrow? I've gotta go out Wednesday. I'm helping build a set for the Christmas play at the church."

"You sure that's okay? Morgan won't mind or anything?"

Sophie pictured Eileen and the major crisis that would result if she asked somebody home for dinner on such short notice.

Tessa shook her head. "She won't care. She's not like that."

Sophie thought of her father and his strict rules, and her face fell. "I'll have to ask my dad first, though. He's grounded me for the rest of my natural life."

"I bet he won't mind. He knows us. He's been over to the house a coupla times. Him and Morgan actually went out on a date last Friday, did ya know that?" She rolled her eyes and giggled. "He was so cute, your dad. He brought flowers and chocolates, like in one of those old movies." She scribbled on a paper napkin, missing Sophie's shocked reaction to her casual revelation. "Here's my number. Call, okay?"

Her father had gone out on a date with this Morgan?

Sophie watched Tessa hurry off and then slowly got to her feet and put on her coat. A tumult of emotions boiled inside her. She felt more left out and alone than ever, betrayed and hurt by the news that her father had taken somebody out and she hadn't even known.

Of course she knew he was really good-looking—she'd seen lots of women coming on to him. And she understood about sex and people's needs. Mummy had been gone four years now and her dad wasn't a monk, after all. So what did she expect?

She expected him to understand about Jason. She expected him to pay some attention to her instead of being gone all the time. She expected him to mention it if he was dating somebody.

Fighting back tears, she walked slowly to the bus stop. It was getting late and she was tired, but more than ever before she hated going home. The house would be empty: Eileen had computer class and her father had said he had a meeting, but now Sophie wondered if he was actually somewhere with this Morgan.

Life was such a mess. She wasn't allowed to see Jason, but her dad could spend time with somebody if he wanted. Was that fair? And that somebody had to be Tessa's foster mom, of all people. Just when she thought she'd made a friend, her dad had to mess everything up, as usual.

The bus came and she got on, thinking of Tessa.

Eileen would totally freak when she laid eyes on her, what with the purple hair and the rings and the makeup, which was reason enough to be friends with her even if Sophie didn't really like her. Which she did. *Really.*

Most of all, though, she wanted to meet Morgan. She had a right to know who her own father was dating, didn't she?

NORMALLY MORGAN FLOPPED onto any horizontal surface and slept until she was awakened by either an alarm or a telephone, a legacy from her days as an intern. But ever since her date with Luke, she hadn't been sleeping well.

She'd spent part of Saturday and Sunday nights drifting in a sensual fog, recalling every kiss, every caress, every sensation her body had registered, and Monday night followed the same pattern. Instead of the dose of cold reality she'd expected to occur once she was away from Luke's seductive presence, she found herself regretting that circumstance hadn't allowed matters to take their natural course.

After all, she was thirty-six years old, she told herself as a chilly dawn finally broke outside her bedroom window. She was enough of a realist to know that an affair with Luke wasn't about to end with a wedding. So what harm could it do to allow her sensuality an opportunity to flower?

She got up and showered, pleased with the way the new haircut fell into place with the touch of a brush, and she decided to put on one of the outfits Tessa had insisted they buy on their shopping trip—black leggings with a long black turtleneck tunic. Tessa said it was just the thing to wear under a lab coat, and she'd made Morgan buy half a dozen variations of it. Morgan laced up the soft leather ankle boots she'd fallen in love with and looked at herself in the mirror.

Wow! Was this really her? She liked the effect, but she didn't look like the Morgan she was used to, that was for sure. The outfit was as comfortable as her old cords, but she looked like one of those polished women who actually coordinated their wardrobe.

Downstairs, Tessa admired her from every angle, extravagantly pleased with the look she'd orchestrated.

"How'd your meeting go last night?" Morgan stuck bread in the toaster, delighted that Tessa seemed so happy.

"Not bad. There weren't as many people there as Frannie hoped, though. You know you told me to watch for Doc Gilbert's daughter?"

Morgan had told Tessa in strictest confidence about Sophie. "She was at the meeting? That's great."

"Yeah. I got talking to her. She's really cute. I asked her over for supper tonight if that's okay. I'll come home right after school and make that noodle stuff you showed me and some cookies. You don't mind, eh?''

"Not at all.'' Morgan was surprised, however, and when she thought about it, pleased. Tessa had never invited a girlfriend for supper before. How nice that she and Luke's daughter had hit it off.

"I've told you you're welcome to ask your friends over whenever you like.'' Morgan wondered if Luke might want to come, too. Would that be a good idea? She buttered her toast and ate it, mulling over the idea.

She didn't know where this thing with her and him was going, but she assumed they were friends. Which she figured meant becoming involved in each other's lives, didn't it? But did it include getting together over a makeshift meal with Tessa and Sophie?

Morgan had no idea. She'd have to talk it over with him. There was so much they didn't know about each other. There were a zillion questions she wanted to ask him. The prospect pleased her.

"Hey, Earth to Morgan.'' Tessa was grinning at her, and it was obvious she'd said something Morgan hadn't even heard.

"Sorry, Tess. I was someplace else.''

"I'll say you were. I said, if you're leaving now, think I could get a ride? I need to get to school early to work on my art project.''

"Sure. Let's go."

Tessa grabbed her bag, and they were halfway out the back door when the front doorbell rang. Major started barking.

"I'll get it. It's pro'bly the mailman." Tessa sprinted through the kitchen and down the hallway to the door. Through the noise of the dogs, Morgan heard Tessa greet whoever was there, telling the animals to shut up at regular intervals.

Tessa hollered, "Hey, Morgan? I think you better come out here." There was a peculiar note in her voice.

Morgan glanced at her watch, muttered under her breath and hurried down the hall, coming to an abrupt halt when she rounded the corner and saw the elegant older woman poised in the entrance hall. Almost faint with shock, Morgan sagged against the wall.

"In-India?" Morgan was too dismayed to even be polite. "What the heck are you doing here? I...I thought you were in Florida."

"*Darling,* what a way to greet your *mother.*" India Merriweather, full-length fur coat swinging open to reveal a bone-slender figure set off by a smart rose-shaded suit, swept across the space dividing them and bent regally to not quite touch her cheek to Morgan's. Skippy yapped at her heels and the kitten came bounding out of the kitchen to see what was going on.

"I know it's very naughty of me to just pop in on you this way, but I decided on the spur of the moment to come for a visit, so I just climbed on the first available plane and here I am." India's throaty, dramatic voice made the whole thing sound like a cozy little adventure. "Surely all these animals aren't yours, Morgan? A cat? Oh, dear, cat hairs irritate my sinuses, you know."

The doorbell rang, and again Tessa opened the door.

"Where d'ya want this luggage, ma'am?" A tiny man stood there, puffing hard. He carried three oversize matching suitcases and several hatboxes.

"Oh, just put them anywhere here. The hall is fine," India instructed him with a careless wave of her beringed, manicured fingers. She lowered her voice to a stage whisper and turned again to Morgan. "Would you have change for this nice man, darling? I'm afraid I don't have any Canadian currency at all—so silly of me. The fare's $32.50 and, dear, please give him a generous tip. He was very helpful at the airport." She gave the taxi driver a winning smile and added in a louder tone, "There are three more pieces, aren't there?"

"Yes, ma'am. I'll get them right away." He turned and went down the steps, and when he staggered back up again under the weight of what looked like small trunks, Morgan had found her handbag.

Thank goodness she'd been to the bank machine. She handed over the money, still too stunned to do more than simply react.

When the door closed behind the driver, she tried to take a deep breath and felt as if she were choking. The air was heavy with the familiar exotic scent India had always worn, and her physical presence, as always, made Morgan feel short, dumpy and unattractive. Inadequate.

Tessa had been standing to one side watching, wide-eyed and silent, and now India turned to her, her frosted golden head tipped to one side.

"And who exactly are you, dear?"

The condescension in her mother's tone set Morgan's teeth on edge. "This is Tessa Hargraves, my foster daughter. I'm sure I wrote you about her coming to live with me. This is my mother, Tessa. India Merriweather."

"And you may call me India, Tara."

"It's Tessa, actually."

Morgan caught the irritation in Tessa's tone and applauded the girl's spirit.

"How long are you planning on staying, India?" With growing apprehension, Morgan eyed the small mountain of cases cluttering the entrance hall. Tessa was also staring at the pile. The dogs were circling it and sniffing.

India strolled into the living room and looked around, trailing a hand across the back of the sofa and studying the painting over the fireplace, her head tipped to one side. "Oh, a nice long visit, no set dates. That's too boring, don't you think? I'll stay for Christmas, certainly."

Christmas? *Christmas?* Morgan's mouth dropped open. It wasn't even Halloween, and India was talking about staying till Christmas? This was a nightmare! It couldn't be happening.

"It'll be such fun," India went on, oblivious to Morgan's reaction. "You and I together for the holidays. This house is simply huge! I had no idea. I'm so glad, dear, because this way we won't all be under one another's feet, will we? Tara, I wonder if you'd be a darling and take my cases up for me?"

Tessa narrowed her eyes and didn't move. Morgan glared at her mother's back, wishing she could be rebellious, too.

She wanted to just say no, she didn't have room. No, India couldn't stay. No, a nice long visit would be anything but fun. No, no, *no.*

But she'd never won an argument with India in her life, so instead of confrontation, she chose flight.

CHAPTER ELEVEN

"THE BAGS ARE GOING to have to wait, India. I have to get to work and Tessa's going to be late for school if we don't leave right now."

Morgan herded Tessa ahead of her, talking steadily as she headed for the back door. "Make yourself comfortable. There's coffee in the pot, leftovers in the fridge if you're hungry and my office number's by the phone. I'll try to make it home early, but right now we've got to go." She wrenched open the back door and called over her shoulder, "'Bye."

Morgan shut the door firmly behind her, aware that she was trembling as if she had palsy.

Tessa was silent as Morgan backed the Jeep out of the garage and swung into the street.

"So. So that's your mother, huh?" The girl's voice was carefully casual. "She sorta still looks like a movie star, even if she's kinda old."

"Yeah, she does." Morgan shivered and turned the heater on, knowing the chill in her body had nothing to do with the weather.

"What kind of fur is her coat, d'ya think?"

Morgan shook her head, her mind in a turmoil. "I have no idea. I've never liked fur. I can't tell one kind from another."

Tessa was quiet again. They were nearing the school when she said in a worried tone, "I don't think she liked me very much, Morgan."

Morgan pulled the Jeep to a stop in a bus zone and reached over and gave Tessa a quick, hard hug.

"Well, I like you a lot, so don't let that bother you, Tess. India's just a little hard to get to know."

The real truth was, her mother had never liked Morgan much, either, so there wasn't a lot of hope for Tess, she thought dismally. She was going to nail India down on exactly how long this visit would last, so at least she and Tessa had something to look forward to.

"So, is it still okay to have Sophie come over tonight?"

"Absolutely." Morgan tried to sound more confident than she felt. "Nothing's going to be different just because India's visiting. Our home is our home. We'll make her welcome, but we won't change our life. She's the one who's going to have to fit in. Agreed?"

"Agreed." Tessa was relieved, and she gave Morgan a smile and a thumbs-up signal. "Oops, here comes a bus. He's gonna kill you for parking here. I'm gone. See ya later.'' She slid out of the Jeep.

Morgan pulled back into traffic, wishing she felt as optimistic about India as she'd pretended to Tessa.

She thought of Luke, of asking him to supper and the increased complications of having her mother staying with her for an indefinite amount of time. Her heart sank.

Why, oh why, did India have to turn up now? It was almost as though talking about her at dinner the other night had drawn her, like some evil genie, out of a bottle.

WHEN SHE WAS CERTAIN Morgan and that girl were gone, India slid her arms out of her coat. The damned thing weighed a ton. She dug out one of the vials of pills from her handbag and, with trembling fingers, shoved several tablets under her tongue and waited for them to dissolve.

Feeling weak and faint, she sank into an armchair and dabbed at the moisture on her forehead and neck with a tissue. Her heart was thundering erratically in her chest, and the ever-present fear swelled inside of her like an overfilled balloon ready to burst. Would death come like this, when she was alone and afraid?

Congestive cardiomyopathy. Very musical. At

least it sounded suitably elegant and extraordinary. And if she had to die, she'd rather it wasn't cancer. Cancer was too common, really. Everyone in Hollywood was doing cancer or AIDS.

The diseases had something in common, though. There wasn't any real cure for any of them. Rest, sleep, avoid stress, the young cardiologist had said. And pills, of course. India made a face. She had an entire makeup case filled with pills, for all the good they did.

Perhaps another year if you take very good care of yourself, he'd said when India insisted, but his eyes had said otherwise. Of course doctors always exaggerated how much time you had left; they didn't want to take away hope.

Just not right now, in this strange house, with Morgan not here....

With a supreme effort of will, India forced herself to do the breathing exercises she'd used as an actress when stage fright threatened to get the better of her.

In...out—deep into the diaphragm, even though it hurt, oh, God it hurt. In...out.

In slow increments, the panic and pain subsided.

"Get away. Go away! I don't like cats." The kitten was winding itself around her ankle, and India shoved at it with her toe. She realized it had only one eye and shuddered.

Irritation took the place of fear as India looked around the room. It was pleasant enough. Morgan had some quite nice pieces.

The two dogs were lying on the rug, staring at her with their tails wagging. One of them had something wrong with its leg. The other was making a peculiar sound, somewhere between a bark and a whine. Heaven only knew what it had wrong with it.

Why Morgan would clutter up a perfectly lovely old house with crippled and blind animals was beyond her comprehension. And that cheap-looking girl with the purple spikes for hair! What was Morgan thinking of? She was a doctor. Didn't she realize she had a position to uphold in the community?

My daughter, the doctor. It always sent a thrill of pride through her, although it was unfortunate her daughter hadn't inherited her own looks and height. It was difficult to remember Morgan's father clearly—so much water under the bridge since then—but she thought he'd had auburn hair, not brick red, and India was fairly certain he'd been tall. All her husbands were, so where Morgan had inherited that tiny stature was beyond her. At least the girl had gotten her brains, she concluded with smug complacence.

She decided she felt well enough to get up and climb very slowly up the stairs to find out what her room was going to be like. One of the dogs, the small black poodle, followed her in spite of what she said to it.

Upstairs she assessed the situation and concluded that Morgan had selfishly claimed the best and largest bedroom. And the second-best room was obviously that girl's, with pictures of half-naked rock stars and sullen young men on motorcycles all over the walls.

The third room she inspected was for a baby. It had a rocking chair and a wooden crib and a small white wardrobe.

India stood in the doorway and frowned. Had Morgan gone totally broody and decided to adopt a baby? Or, God forbid, have one of her own? A lot of young women were doing that now, heaven only knew why. One pregnancy had been quite enough for her, thank you.

That left one last bedroom. It was small and the bed was ridiculous—far too narrow—but at the moment it would have to do. She thought longingly of the queen-size bed in the trailer she'd sold in Florida, but what was done was done. She'd lived her life without indulging in regrets, and she wouldn't start now. The money had paid her medical expenses and her plane fare.

Surely Morgan would see the sense of putting that girl in here and letting India have the larger room, she decided as she found sheets and a comforter in the hall cupboard and made up the bed, stopping several times to sit and rest.

Even so, she was exhausted and breathless by the time she finished. The cheapest flight from Florida had involved flying all night, and she had no reserves of energy to draw on.

She fumbled her way out of her clothing, forcing herself to hang it all up carefully in the closet before allowing herself to sink down on the bed.

As long as she got enough rest, she could probably postpone telling Morgan about her heart, for a while at least. India hated the idea of anyone feeling sorry for her. And as for the rest of it, the fact that she planned to live here with Morgan for what remained of her life... Well, she'd break that news when she felt like it.

The little black dog jumped up on the bed. It paid no attention when she ordered it off. It settled near her pillow and watched her. She scowled at it, drew the comforter up to her chin, closed her eyes and was instantly asleep.

THE DAY WAS FRANTIC, and by three that afternoon Morgan still hadn't managed to break for lunch. She finished with one patient and was checking the next chart when Luke tapped on the door.

"You busy?"

"Oh, no, I'm just sitting here filing my nails. Want me to do yours?" She grinned at him, and he came in and closed the door. She'd tried to call him earlier, but he'd been delivering a baby at St. Joe's. "How'd your case go?"

"Really well. A fine boy. The mother has three girls at home, so he was a welcome change." He smiled and her heart skipped a beat. "There's a play in the west end I've heard is good. I know it's short notice, but if I can get tickets for tonight, would you like to go?"

"Gosh, I'd like nothing better, but I can't, Luke. My mother arrived with no warning just as I was leaving for work, and I have to go home and get her settled."

She debated about whether or not to ask, and now she made up her mind. "Actually, I wondered if you'd like to come over for supper tonight. It seems Tessa invited your daughter. They met at that meeting last night and hit it off. The meal won't be anything fancy, but I just thought maybe..." Her voice trailed away.

He was looking at her, his expression unreadable, and she felt suddenly embarrassed and annoyed with herself for asking him in the first place. "Look, it's a terrible idea. Forget I said anything."

He shook his head. "It's not. It's very kind

of you. You caught me off guard. Sophie didn't say anything this morning about meeting Tessa." He hesitated and then added, "It might be awkward, me coming along, because as I told you, Sophie and I don't get on well these days. I haven't mentioned to her that I'm seeing you socially. And there's a chance she'll feel I'm intruding."

"Well, think it over. But India and I don't get on well, either, so at least you and I could talk to each other when the parental thing turns nasty. If you want to come, that is."

He hesitated again and then nodded. "I do. I'd like to meet your mother, Morgan. From what you've told me, she's an interesting woman."

Morgan rolled her eyes. "See if you can hold that thought after you've been around her a couple of hours. We'll eat about seven if that's okay with you."

The intercom on her desk sounded, and Rachel's dictatorial voice said, "Mrs. Parsons is waiting in Room 3, Doctor. She says to remind you that she's been there for twenty minutes now."

Morgan rolled her eyes. "Gotta go. Rachel's on the warpath, not to mention Mrs. Parsons."

"Not so fast." He moved closer and drew her

to him for a quick, hard kiss. "I'm working on our problem. I'll have it solved in a day or two."

"Our problem? Oh, *that* problem." Morgan could feel herself flush when she realized he was talking about a place where they could be alone together. Make love together.

"Good," she managed to answer, and for the rest of the afternoon, she could think of little else except what Luke had in mind.

INDIA DRESSED FOR DINNER in a soft peach-colored turtleneck sweater, wide-legged black silk trousers and ridiculously high-heeled black sandals. She had more impressive-looking jewelry draped on her ears, neck, wrists and fingers than Morgan and Tessa owned jointly.

They'd had no time to wash their faces, let alone change.

India looked at them both and sniffed. "Leggings?"

She was even more horrified when she learned they'd be eating at the kitchen table. Morgan explained that she hadn't gotten around to buying a dining room table yet, feeling the familiar sense of inadequacy India always inspired.

Then there were the hors d'ouevres, a bag of tortilla chips dumped unceremoniously into a bowl, served with a dish of salsa, the hot type Tess and Morgan preferred. India was scandalized. This, Morgan thought, from a woman whose idea of dinner had been to have her small daughter open a can of soup. Morgan had learned to cook in self-defense.

When Luke and Sophie first walked through the front door, Morgan felt a burst of total panic. It was obvious from Sophie's sullen face and Luke's set jaw that father and daughter weren't on the best of terms, and India had managed to make Tessa furious by criticizing the noodle casserole the girl was so proud of. It looked as if the evening was going to be a disaster, and Morgan's fears intensified when Luke introduced his daughter.

"I'm delighted to meet you, Sophie." Morgan took the girl's hand in both her own and smiled in welcome.

Sophie gave her a suspicious, narrow-eyed look and jerked her hand away.

With the animals, however, she was entirely different. She got down on her hands and knees on the rug and greeted each dog with a hug as Tess gave her a rundown on their personalities and peculiar traits. She actually giggled when Skippy lay down on his back and waved his legs in the air in a fit of his usual dementia.

Once the initial awkwardness was over, Luke was soon smiling, as well—in fact, Morgan was amazed to hear him laugh aloud several times at things India said to him. Morgan had forgotten the way her mother turned on her charm the moment a handsome male was around.

India had complained nonstop since the moment Morgan walked in the door a scant hour ago. Now, she was suddenly smiling and full of gracious compliments and flirtatious glances as she allowed Luke to pour her a glass of wine from the bottle he'd brought.

The two of them settled on the sofa while Morgan went out to the kitchen to help put the finishing touches on the simple meal Tessa had prepared.

"Can I help you, Tess?" Sophie had followed Tessa to the kitchen and was studiously ignoring Morgan.

"Sure. You can wash the lettuce for the salad. You like to cook, Soph?" Tessa was removing her noodle casserole from the oven, oven mitts on her hands and a concentrated expression on her face.

"I've never tried, really. Eileen—that's Daddy's housekeeper—she doesn't like for me to be in the kitchen." There was no mistaking the antipathy in Sophie's tone when she said Eileen's name. "She says I make too much of a mess."

"Morgan says messes are just part of cooking, right, Morgan?" Tessa was clearly showing off, arranging snips of parsley as decoration on the top of the noodles with all the finesse of a master chef. "You should taste these chocolate-chip cookies I make from Morgan's secret recipe. You put in candy and it melts and goes all gooey. I was gonna make 'em tonight but I didn't have time."

Morgan knew why. Tess had told her the moment she came home from school she'd been railroaded by India into taking all her luggage up to her room, helping her unpack, finding her extra hangers, even clearing shelves in both bathrooms for India's copious cosmetics. On top of that, India had tried to force Tess to trade bedrooms with her.

"She thinks I'm a maid or something," Tess had whispered with tears of anger and frustration in her eyes, and Morgan had wanted to strangle her mother before she'd even said ten words to her. "I'll set her straight," Morgan had promised, embarrassed and furious.

"Why don't the two of you make up a batch of those cookies after supper," Morgan suggested now to the girls. "They don't take long."

Sophie forgot to be aloof. "*Alll right.* Could we really?"

"Sure." Tessa grinned at her. "We got all the stuff—it'll be fun."

"Super," Sophie breathed, as if making cookies was a major event in her life. "I used to do

that with my mom before she died.'' She
glanced at Morgan. ''She was such a great cook,
my mom. She used to make this apple pie you
cook in a paper bag. It was awesome! My dad
used to say she was the best cook in the world.
And birthday cakes—she made me one once that
had a castle on top, with a princess in a tower
and all these turrets and things. And she was
really tall and pretty, my mom. She could play
the piano.''

Morgan listened, nodded and smiled, and it
dawned on her that Sophie was listing her mother's talents for her benefit. The girl obviously
knew there was something between Morgan and
her father and was making it plain she wasn't
happy about it, Morgan deduced.

So for the rest of the evening, Morgan used
every ounce of her warmth and charm in an all-
out effort to win Sophie's trust and friendship.

If she could avoid it, she wasn't going to be
the source of any more conflict between Luke
and his daughter.

CHAPTER TWELVE

"THAT WAS A pleasant evening." Luke pulled the car to a stop at a light and glanced at his daughter. She hadn't said anything since they'd left Morgan's a few moments before, but she seemed less guarded than usual. "You and Tessa get on very well."

"Yeah. She's okay." Sophie's tone was neutral and cool, but at least they were having some semblance of a conversation, and Luke was grateful not to have his head bitten off.

Privately, he had a lot of reservations about Tessa. He remembered all too clearly the evidence of physical violence on her body when her baby was born and Morgan's disturbing assessment of Dylan, the baby's father. The last thing Luke wanted was his daughter involved with members of a street gang, but he had enough sense to know that this wasn't the time for cautionary lectures.

"I liked those cookies you girls made. Maybe you could make us a batch at home."

"Humph. That'd be the day." Tessa's voice

was scathing. "Eileen would never let me. You know what she's like about the kitchen. She thinks it's a hospital or something."

"From what I know of hospitals, Eileen's way off base if she figures they're a standard for cleanliness." It was a lame joke at best, but it felt good when she smiled. It encouraged Luke to say something he'd been thinking of broaching with her. "You don't like Eileen much, do you, Soph?"

She was silent but she shook her head from side to side with vehemence, and her expression said more than words would have.

"Well, maybe we ought to let her go and find a housekeeper we both get along with," he ventured. It had been on his mind ever since Morgan had suggested it.

Sophie's head pivoted toward him. "Oh, Daddy, could we really?" Her voice was filled with such longing that Luke made up his mind then and there.

"I'll give her notice tomorrow morning. But this time I want you to do the interviewing and the hiring."

"You mean it?"

"Absolutely."

"Oh, Daddy, thank you." Sophie reached over and touched his arm, and he silently sent Morgan a huge thank-you. Then he took a deep breath and dared to add, "And if you still are determined to have your baby, you ought to think of hiring someone who's a bit more flexible than Eileen, someone you feel comfortable talking with."

"I will, because I'm keeping it." Sophie's voice was both fervent and defiant, but when Luke didn't object, she added in a shy tone that made his heart swell, "I think babies are pretty messy, so we'll need somebody really easygoing. And, Daddy?"

"What, Soph?" It was the best conversation they'd had in months, and he felt warm inside and eager for it to continue.

"I'm changing doctors." Again there was defiance in her voice. "That lady you sent me to is okay, I guess, but I decided tonight I want Morgan to deliver my baby. I really like Morgan."

He did, too, far more than Sophie knew, but the thought of her becoming so intimately involved with his daughter was disconcerting. He'd planned to keep Morgan as separate as possible from the rest of his life, and somehow it wasn't working. Dinner tonight had been pleasant, but it had brought complications, just as he'd feared it might.

"If that's what you want, I'll speak to her about it."

"I'm perfectly capable of speaking to her about it myself, Daddy." The frostiness was back in Sophie's voice. Luke sighed and they made the rest of the trip in silence, but for the first time in weeks he didn't have the painful feeling that his daughter totally despised him, even though she was still deeply angry with him.

He thought about what Morgan had said about anger, that it was often a cover for sadness.

If that was so, then Sophie had good reason for her anger. She wasn't having a carefree adolescence by any means, poor kid. He vowed he'd somehow learn how to be a better father to her.

And what about his own anger, the rage he felt toward Jason, the cold fury that came over him whenever he thought about Deborah?

Strangely enough, the intensity of those emotions wasn't constant anymore. There had even been moments tonight when he'd felt light-hearted and happy.

He didn't admit that those moments had a lot to do with Morgan.

WHEN INDIA AND TESSA were in bed that night and the kitchen was more or less tidy, Morgan sat down in front of the fireplace with the lights out, Major at her feet and the kitten in a warm, furry mound on her lap. For some inexplicable reason, Skippy had followed India upstairs.

Morgan stared into the flames and wondered why the evening had left her feeling so grumpy. It had actually gone much better than it might have, she reminded herself. Tessa had glowed when Luke complimented her on the casserole. India had outdone herself in her role of femme fatale. The girls had enjoyed making cookies, and Sophie had actually giggled with pleasure when Luke bit into one and pretended to swoon. Then she'd chatted with Morgan, and when they were alone in the kitchen, confided that her baby had moved for the first time.

Everyone laughed when Major, for some obscure reason of his own, tried to climb into Luke's lap. Luke and Sophie had seemed much more relaxed with each other by the time they left, and Luke had given Morgan a secret, lewd wink that made her heart hammer just before he followed Sophie out to his car.

Apart from that one gesture, there hadn't been a single other opportunity for a private word or an intimate moment between them, but Morgan hadn't expected one anyway, not with the girls and India present.

India. Morgan scowled and banged her empty cup down on the arm of the chair, sloshing coffee grounds on the already stained upholstery. India drove her nuts. Her mother was the sore spot, Morgan admitted, the reason she felt cranky and out of sorts.

It was embarrassing to have to admit even to herself, but she was a little jealous of the courtly attention Luke had paid India tonight, disgruntled by the way the two of them seemed to get along so well and find things to talk about. She and her mother had never had anything in common, apart from the accident of birth, so it was disconcerting for Morgan to acknowledge that Luke seemed to have found India entertaining and interesting.

The simple fact was, Morgan resented having her mother intrude in her life this way. Her life was her creation, she mused bitterly. It had taken enormous dedication and backbreaking work to get to where she was, with a steady job she adored, earning her a good income, a home of her own, beloved pets, a foster daughter she cherished. For the first time in her life, she had a measure of self-confidence, a sense of her own worth. Even, miraculously, a man she cared for, and although she reminded herself that was only temporary, she wanted to enjoy every minute with Luke while it lasted.

Until now, India had never once made an effort to be part of Morgan's life. Her own life had always been much too important to her. In all the years Morgan had been in Canada, India had never before made the effort to come and visit, even missing Morgan's graduation from med school. Her mother had been holidaying with a friend in Mexico.

So the big question was, why on earth had she turned up here now? And why the heck was she being so vague about the length of her stay? Morgan knew her mother well enough to know that India never did anything unless there was an advantage in it for her.

Well, there was no point sitting up half the night worrying about it, because undoubtedly she'd find out sooner or later. Yawning, Morgan made certain the screen was in front of the fire and encouraged Major to go out before bed.

Tomorrow was going to be another busy day, which she always enjoyed, and there was the added pleasure of knowing she'd talk to Luke.

Thinking of him and wishing he was there in her bed, she trailed up the stairs.

"MORGAN?" LUKE'S VOICE was warm and intimate in her ear. It was late the following afternoon, and she realized that some tiny part of her had been waiting all day to hear from him.

"If you're done seeing patients, how about coming for a ride with me? There's something I want to show you. I could pick you up in fifteen minutes."

She thought of India waiting at home with a list of the day's complaints and expecting someone to make her a meal. There'd be just the two of them, Morgan thought with dread. Tessa was working on the stage set at the church, and she'd called to say she was having a burger with some friends.

"Fifteen minutes is fine," she said into the receiver. She'd call her mother and tell her to open a can of soup or something, and she would *not* feel guilty about it.

When Luke's car stopped at the curb outside the clinic, Morgan was waiting on the sidewalk, anticipation swelling inside her. She had a hunch he'd solved their problem.

"Isn't it a great afternoon?" Motor running, Luke reached across and opened the passenger door and she got in. The next thing she knew, he'd slid an arm around her and pulled her as close as he could, considering the gear shift. He pressed a quick and urgent kiss on her mouth. His good humor seemed to envelop her in warmth.

He was smiling when he let her go, and she realized he was dressed more casually than she'd ever seen him, in a pair of jeans that molded his lean hips and powerful thighs, and a navy sweater underneath a brown leather jacket. She looked at his hands on the steering wheel as he pulled away from the curb. They were large hands, strong and shapely, long fingered and graceful, and all she could think of was how they'd feel on her body.

Get a grip, Jacobsen. You're turning into a lecherous woman here.

LUKE STEPPED HARD on the gas, sending the powerful little car shooting into the heavy stream of traffic. He wondered how to tell her his news and then decided to just say it. After all, it had been her idea, in a way.

"Morgan, I've subleased a houseboat. It's permanently moored in False Creek. I saw it on the electronic bulletin board at the hospital. It belongs to one of the surgeons, but he and his wife are going off to work for UNICEF for two years. They used it as a weekend hideaway, and it's fully furnished—linens, dishes, everything. He was anxious to get it rented because they're leaving next week, so we slipped off to the real estate office and signed the papers an hour ago."

Feeling elated and very pleased with himself, he slid between a bus and a taxi and then sped up to make it through a yellow light. "I confess I haven't actually seen it yet myself. I hope it's as good as advertised."

He glanced over at her, and the hunger he felt was urgent. He noted the high color in her cheeks and the way the long green sweater she wore clung to her full breasts. Green was a good color for her.

His voice dropped to an intimate level. "The truth is, I wanted you with me. I picked up some supplies, and I thought we'd have a picnic on board."

He took an off-ramp from the bridge and wound rapidly down the streets that led to False Creek, pulling into the parking area with a flourish.

"The boats are parked just along the quay. We're number 612."

He bolted out of the car and hurried around to open Morgan's door. The winter sun was just going down over the North Shore mountains, and the air was cold and bracing. He couldn't remember the last time he'd felt so full of excitement and anticipation.

Morgan was being uncharacteristically quiet, Luke noted as he set the bags of food on the counter in the houseboat's tiny kitchen and opened the cupboard doors one after the other looking for glasses in which to serve the wine. She'd barely said two words since he'd picked her up.

She was standing by the windows, staring out at the scene of water and mountains that the wraparound view provided.

"There's more space in one of these than you'd think," she commented as he finally found wineglasses in a cupboard tucked away above the compact refrigerator.

"Isn't it fine? I've always fantasized about living on a houseboat," he confessed. He uncorked the wine and poured it, then walked over to her and handed her the glass, but he didn't relinquish it when she reached for it. He held on, forcing her to look up at him.

"Morgan," he said in a quiet voice. "Have I gone too quickly here? Am I making you feel uncomfortable or pressured? Because that wasn't my intention, my dear. I simply thought we could have a pleasant few hours in a private place. We're surrounded by people so much of the time, I'd like for us to be alone together for a change."

She nodded, and he added in a much lighter tone, "Now, I missed lunch and I'm bloody starving. How about you?"

It was exactly the right note, deflecting the tension that had sprung up between them. She relaxed all of a sudden and grinned at him. "I'm always starving. What'd you bring?" She moved over to the counter and poked into the bags. She found plates and bowls and arranged the food, setting it out on the table.

He liked the way she ate, with gusto and honest hunger and no irritating remarks about fat content or calories or the need for dieting. He thought wistfully of Sophie, wishing she'd eat the way Morgan did.

Luke thanked her for having him and Sophie over, and he talked about a mystery he was reading, a spy movie he wanted to see, a patient who'd been referred. They finished the lunch, and he found a coffeepot and brewed some of the special blend he'd bought. Then they took cookies and coffee over to the soft, mouse-colored couch.

"Mmm. This is heaven." Morgan drew her legs up under her and bit into her cookie with the greedy relish that delighted him. She looked like a sexy elf in her leggings and sweater, and once again the unbridled hunger, the need he felt for her, was urgent and intense, but he didn't dare draw her into his arms the way he longed to do. He'd decided to go slowly, taking his cues from her, but damn it all, it was difficult. All he could think of was the bed in the back room.

Morgan finished her cookie and sipped her coffee, leaning back against the cushions, pretending to an ease she was far from feeling. The truth was, she felt far from relaxed. Now that the time had come, she was having a massive nervous attack. Performance anxiety, a sex therapist would label it.

She could sense his nearness in every pore, smell the aftershave he used, feel the warmth coming from his body. And suddenly she, who was born talking, couldn't think what to say to him. She was too overwhelmed by apprehension, and Luke certainly wasn't helping her out with conversation.

He was silent, lounging not three feet away, one long leg bent and propped on the other knee, an arm stretched indolently across the back of the sofa, his hand gently touching her shoulder.

She longed to move into the curve of that arm, feel him draw her close. She wanted it badly, and at the same time she wished she had the strength to move away. She could feel each thick, heavy beat of her heart, sluggish and full, and blood seemed to pool in her abdomen.

Holy toot! She was way out of her league here. How did other women deal with attraction this intense? She felt irritated and off balance, irrationally annoyed at him for just sitting there and not saying or doing anything. Couldn't he sense her discomfort? Now that there was a bed, she thought with mounting panic, she was scared to use it.

"Is there any music?" Desperate and breathless, she bolted to her feet and opened cabinets, discovering a built-in stereo system behind louvered doors. "This place is really well equipped, isn't it?'' she babbled. ''The owners must hate to leave it. I would if it was mine.'' She flicked switches at random and chanced on a local FM station that played nonstop ballads. She felt relieved beyond measure to have something besides her own voice filling the heavy silence.

''Dance with me?'' He'd gotten up without her being aware of it, and she turned, half panicked, and found herself already in his arms.

CHAPTER THIRTEEN

"BUT LUKE, I'm not very good at this, I never was. I can't dance...."

Morgan's strangled objections trailed away as his arm came around her and he captured her hand in his. They both knew she wasn't really talking about dancing at all.

"It's fairly simple." He sounded amused. "Put your hand on my shoulder, like this. Now lean against me and move your feet a little." He was smiling down at her. "And you're going to have to loosen up just a bit. Try to relax."

She could tell this was something he did really well. She thought he was making fun of her, and his amusement and the way her senses reacted to his nearness made her temper flare. "Well, some of us didn't have fancy dancing lessons when we were young," she snapped.

"Right. Some of us didn't," he agreed in a mild tone, guiding her so firmly she could hardly go wrong, and yet she did. "The history master at school taught the lot of us boys one Saturday afternoon. He was sixty-two at the time, and I was twelve, so I'd say my technique's more than a bit outdated.''

"Outdated, newfangled, what the heck do I know?'' she growled, and then tromped on his instep so hard that he winced. "Sorry, sorry.'' Feeling mortified, she tried to draw away, but he wouldn't let her.

"Close your eyes and just let go, my dear,'' he ordered, drawing her even tighter into his embrace, holding her firmly against his hip. "Pretend you're delivering a baby, working with the contractions. That's dancing.''

She did, and she felt his rhythm in her bones. Suddenly she was dancing, matching his every step, floating along to the music, every dip and whirl and turn synchronized.

The heels on her boots brought the top of her head to just under his chin, and after a few giddy moments, she dared to nestle there, enchanted with the way she was able to anticipate his every move and respond.

Delighted, she giggled a little. Flap Jacobsen, total klutz when it came to anything coordinated, had discovered a newfound grace that amazed and delighted her.

The music changed, the tempo quickened, and still she followed him, breathless, drunk with the simple joy of movement, of being close to him in such total harmony.

And then the music slowed again, to the lonely wail of a saxophone. Morgan realized through a fog of pleasure that they were swaying in place, barely moving at all. Her arms had snaked around his neck, and her breasts were pressed against him. Her breathing quickened, and she could feel his heart against her cheek, thrumming deep and hard and insistent. She could also feel his arousal, and her own body throbbed in response.

He moved his hand from where it was spread across the small of her back. He touched her face with his fingertips, stroking her cheek and then under her chin, tipping her head up so she was looking into his smoldering eyes.

"Morgan, I need to love you."

A shuddering breath caught in her throat, and before she could expel it, he'd bent and claimed her lips.

His taste was familiar and dear. Their tongues met in a shivery dance, and with a groan he tilted his head, deepening the kiss, angling this way and that in a caress that was soon out of control. His tongue thrust in and out, his lips nuzzled, his teeth nipped at her swollen bottom lip.

"Let me touch you." His hands slid beneath her tunic, touching bare skin, gliding up her ribs until his palms found her breasts.

"I've wanted to touch you this way for so long," he breathed, moving his hands in maddening, slow circles until her nipples strained against the lacy bra that enclosed them.

She trembled and burned, pressing herself against him, and their mouths devoured each other. His clever fingers unloosed the clasp on her bra, and at last her naked flesh rested in his palms.

He kissed her, murmuring something frantic into her mouth and cupping her aching breasts, taking the sensitive nipples between thumb and forefinger, gently rubbing, fueling the burning desire that threatened to overwhelm her.

He slid his hands down to her bottom, cupping and lifting her. Heat and need burned low in her belly, and she ground herself against his swollen body.

"Dangerous, my love," he muttered, tension in every syllable. He slid her down, and she groaned in dismay when her feet touched the carpet, unsure whether she could even stand on her own. Then he was peeling the tunic up and over her head, tearing the straps of her bra down her arms and off, and all she could feel was relief at becoming free of the constraint of clothing.

"Morgan, you are so beautiful." Luke's eyes were on her breasts, and then his lips closed over a nipple, suckling, drawing and releasing. Sensation rippled through her, bringing a gasp of pleasure.

He knelt, sliding her leggings and panties down, stopping to caress her buttocks and press hot, slow kisses in the nest of curls at the apex of her thighs until her knees gave way and she had to lean on his shoulders to support herself.

He muttered in frustration when he encountered her laced boots, but it was only a matter of seconds before he had them undone and off her feet and at last she stood naked before him. He got up, and together they tore at his clothing until it lay scattered with hers.

She was aware of his naked body, of the lean, supple strength and perfect proportions that his clothing only hinted at. He was beautiful, flat bellied, long limbed and graceful, and she was suddenly self-conscious in her own nakedness.

Most of the time, except when she was around India, of course, she was at home in her body, perfectly comfortable with her tiny, full-breasted frame, but it had been years since she'd been naked with a man. She reached for the tunic lying on the floor, but he restrained her.

"Don't do that," he whispered. "Let me look at you. You're so small, so perfect." He slid his hands down her body, his eyes worshiping every lush curve.

"Morgan." His voice was unrecognizable, thick and rasping, out of control. "Put your arms around my neck."

He carried her effortlessly down the short hallway and into the bedroom. He lowered her to the bed and she trembled, filled with fierce, wild sexual hunger.

"Morgan, are you protected?"

She nodded. She'd seen to it after their first date.

In a fever of need, she felt his hard, heated flesh between her wet thighs.

"Don't want to hurt you," he gasped, and she sensed he was holding back.

"Luke, let go. Love me. Just love me." She was half sobbing with need, and she grabbed his shoulders, pulling him down to her, wrapping her legs around him and writhing with desire.

"My sweet Morgan." In a single long burning thrust he entered her, jolting her body back against the mattress and driving everything out of her head except the frantic thought that if he stopped now she would die.

Pressure built and built, and she cried out, gripping his back, frantically urging him to drive deeper, harder, until at last pleasure burst in her with such a rush of heat and ecstasy she thought she would shatter like glass.

He caught her scream with his mouth, taking

it into himself as her body convulsed, and the deep pulsating that racked her in turn brought an animal cry to his lips as his own orgasm began. He heaved and surged, and the pressure of his seed shooting into her renewed the spasms that had only moments before convulsed her, bringing her again to a peak of blind sensation that climaxed in a second surge of almost unbearable pleasure, leaving her trembling and gasping and boneless.

He collapsed, careful not to crush her, his damp body half covering hers, his face buried in the soft skin of her shoulder, his gasps slowly subsiding.

Her heartbeat gradually slowed and the delicious aftershocks that trembled through her faded, but it was still a long time before she could think.

When she could, she was stupefied at the scope of her own ignorance.

She was thirty-six. She'd coped with birth and death. She was an obstetrician, a doctor who dealt every day of her working life with issues surrounding women's bodies, women's sexuality. She knew her way blindfolded around the human body, male as well as female; she'd excelled at anatomy and physiology. Yet, in spite of all that, until right now she'd been as ignorant of the fathomless potential of her own sexuality as any virgin, and it astounded her.

"Luke?" She needed to tell him what she was feeling. "You awake?"

"Mmm." He raised his head and looked at her, his eyes dazed and sleepy. He propped himself on an elbow and nibbled kisses across her face and down her neck, and to her amazement his voice was husky and apologetic.

"I'm sorry I was rough, love. I didn't have any control left. Your skin's like silk. It's a wonder I didn't bruise you, taking you like a savage."

"I wanted to be taken that way."

"Oh, Morgan." He kissed her nose. "Have I told you that I love your freckles?"

"I knew it. You're a sexual deviant." She giggled and slid a hand down his length, and his body responded. "I'm so glad."

SHE DROVE HIM MAD. Luke fought for control as she whispered his name and moved her pelvis. He clenched his teeth and held back, which should have been easy this time but wasn't.

Her skin was fiery hot, and the intoxicating taste of her was on his tongue. She was more than he'd ever fantasized a lover could be— innocently sensual, honestly greedy, a little

clumsy, endlessly curious and wholly enchant-
ing.

Morgan...

Everything about her delighted him—the size
and weight of her rounded breasts, their delicate
nipples, the perfect shape of her buttocks, the
slenderness of her waist, the surprising length of
her legs.

But those things were physical. There was
something else that drew him to her, something
intangible, something purely and simply Morgan.

She cried out and her fingers scrabbled across
his back, and he let go. With his own powerful
release came the conviction that this was something he'd never found before, but when he regained his senses, of course he dismissed the
thought. This was sex, pure and simple. This
houseboat would be their private world, their escape from reality.

Each of them had complicated lives. He'd realized last night, talking to her mother, listening
to Tessa, watching Sophie, that those complications could destroy everything if he and Morgan became involved on any other level but this
one.

He had to keep that clear in his mind.

NOVEMBER CAME, and the weather turned nasty,
with steady days of drizzling rain that seemed to

permeate everything with dampness.

Tessa shivered as she slid her key into the lock and opened the back door as quietly as she could. It was almost two in the morning, and her heart sank as she realized there was a light on in the other room. She suddenly felt tense and guilty, even though she knew Morgan wouldn't be sitting there just waiting to tear into her. Morgan never did things like that, but all the same, Tessa knew that tonight she'd broken their bond of trust, and Morgan would be disappointed in her.

When Tess had first come to live here, Morgan hadn't set many rules, which surprised her at first. Instead, they'd talked together and worked out a sort of honor code that Tessa had pretty much stuck with. It was based on mutual honesty and respect, and one of the things they'd agreed to was that if Tess was going to be out really late, she'd call so Morgan wouldn't worry about her.

Well, she hadn't done it tonight. Anyhow, Tess told herself defiantly, Morgan had been out a lot lately, herself. She probably didn't know or even care that Tessa hadn't called home.

Gathering her defenses around her like armor, Tess walked through the kitchen into the living room, relieved and then resentful that it was India who sat under the reading lamp with her manicure case in her satin-covered lap. Skippy was curled up beside her, which further irritated Tessa. The little dog had attached himself to India, and he followed her everywhere these days.

"Hi," Tess said in a sullen tone. "What're you doing up?" It had only been a week since India's arrival, but it seemed like a year. It was a constant struggle for Tess to be polite to the old woman. Everything had changed since she'd come to stay, and Tess had known within a couple of days of having her around that there was no way she'd ever get along with Morgan's mother.

More than anything, Tess thought, she wanted things to return to the way they'd been; she just wanted India to go back where she belonged and stay there.

"What am *I* doing up? *I* happen to suffer from insomnia." India held up a hand to check the talonlike nails she'd painted a deep ruby red. The three gold bracelets she wore clanged together.

She was wearing a turquoise negligee with feathery stuff around the neck and hem. Tess thought it was called marabou. She had to admit that India's clothes and jewelry were really something, even though she was a first-class, conceited old bitch.

"The question is, dear girl, what are *you* doing sneaking in at this hour?"

"I'm not sneaking." At least the dislike between them was mutual, Tess concluded. She was sick and tired of trying to be polite to India, too. "And I'm not your dear girl, and I don't have to explain anything to you," she snapped, jutting her chin out defiantly. "I'm going up to bed."

"Looks to me as if you just got out of bed," India purred in a syrupy tone that stopped Tess in her tracks. "First thing you know, young lady, you'll be knocked up all over again. Unless, of course, you're smarter about birth control than you were before. Morgan mentioned that you just got over one pregnancy."

Outrage and anger took Tessa's breath away for an instant, but then the defensive shell she'd developed on the streets kicked in. She forced her voice to sound cool and unemotional. "You're just jealous because nobody's ever gonna want you in the sack anymore, huh, India?"

The jibe hit home. India gasped and jerked as though she'd been punched, and the fancy manicure case crashed to the carpet, spilling bottles and squares of cotton and emery boards.

Skippy leaped up and cowered as if he'd been struck. India patted him and then pressed a hand to her heart, and her face turned so white that for a moment Tessa was genuinely afraid that maybe she was going to have a heart attack or something. But then Tess remembered that the other woman was an actress, so she turned away and strolled nonchalantly up the stairs, determined not to reveal that India had tricked her for a minute there.

At the landing, however, where India couldn't see her, Tess crouched down for a peek at the older woman, but India had gotten up and gone into the kitchen.

Tess could hear the water running in the sink. The old bitch was probably popping some of those pills she had stashed in her dresser drawers. Tess knew there were about ten different vials of them. She was either a drug addict or a health nut, take your choice. She'd wanted to ask Morgan what the pills were for, but that would have meant admitting she'd poked through the old woman's things.

She went on up the stairs and was about to tiptoe past Morgan's bedroom when she realized the door was open and Morgan wasn't in bed, anyway. She was likely at the hospital delivering somebody's kid. People must've been really turned on last spring, because Morgan had been gone almost every night this week.

Something suddenly clicked in Tessa's head,

and she came to an abrupt standstill outside the bathroom.

Morgan was with Sophie's dad! They were in bed somewhere; she'd bet her leather jacket on it. She went into the bathroom and used the toilet, then washed her face and hands, wondering how she could have been so stupid.

Morgan was having an affair. She even looked different, really pretty, sort of glowing, taking care about her hair and wearing the clothes Tessa had chosen. And the reason was, she'd fallen for Doc Gilbert.

Tess went into her room and pulled off her clothes, tugged on her sleep shirt and climbed into bed. She curled into a ball and pulled the duvet up over her shoulders, but her mind wouldn't quit.

The thought of Morgan and Sophie's dad actually *doing* it made her feel kind of queasy. Sure, they'd gone out to dinner that one time, but right after that, India had arrived and things here got crazy. Tess had started staying away rather than dealing with India's never-ending demands.

Then Dylan was waiting for her after school, and he'd said how sorry he was about the baby and that he'd been too bummed out to even come to her funeral. But, he'd reminded Tess, she'd been the one who'd started the fight in the first place. He hadn't meant to hit her that night, but she knew about his temper. He was sorry, real sorry.

Part of Tess knew he was just making excuses, but another crazy part wanted so much to believe him. She was mad at him for what happened about the baby; she hated him for that, but some other part of her still loved him. It was all a humongous mess in her head.

She *owed* Dylan. He'd been her daddy out on the street. She'd tried to forget about him, tried hanging out with the artsy crowd who were building the set at the church, but she felt older than all of them, just like she did with the kids at school. She didn't belong anywhere anymore. She liked Sophie fine, but she couldn't spend every evening with her.

So she'd gone out with Dylan again, to see if maybe she still belonged with him. That's where she'd been tonight, but India was wrong. Tess hadn't had sex with him, even though Dylan tried everything in the book to make her give in.

She hadn't told Morgan about seeing him. She hadn't told Frannie, either; she pretty much knew how they'd react. But it was her life, right? She was the one who was lonely, really horribly lonely since India had come to stay. It didn't feel the same in the house anymore, and that was India's fault, right?

Being here had seemed like a miracle at first, a dream she'd hardly dared believe was happening. She really loved Morgan, but things just weren't working out. They'd started going bad when Kyla got born too soon, and then, when she'd finally started feeling a little better, India turned up.

And now there was Doc Gilbert. What if Morgan decided to marry him or something? What would become of her?

Tess buried her head in the pillow and cried until her nose was stuffy and her head ached, and then finally, too exhausted to cry anymore, she fell asleep.

CHAPTER FOURTEEN

MORGAN SIPPED HER coffee and glanced down at the stack of charts Rachel had just handed her, noting that her next patient that afternoon was Sophie Gilbert.

It would be Sophie's first visit, and Morgan felt a trifle apprehensive about it. Sophie had phoned and asked if Morgan would take her as a patient, and of course Morgan had said yes, she'd be delighted, to come in as soon as possible.

Morgan mentioned Sophie's call to Luke, suspecting that he might have a problem with her attending his daughter. He'd gotten a look on his face that suggested he wasn't entirely happy about it, but all he'd said was that it was Sophie's decision.

Morgan stared down at the file now, frowning. It didn't take a psychic to figure out that Luke would prefer Sophie to consult someone else, someone he wasn't making love to. That was understandable, she supposed. What was starting to bother her was a nagging suspicion that he was also doing his best to discourage any real contact between his family and hers.

Twice Morgan had suggested they take the girls out for a burger, and both times Luke had refused with some flimsy excuse. Morgan had invited Luke and Sophie over on Friday to watch a video and have pizza, and again he'd found a reason why they couldn't come.

Saturday afternoon, Sophie and Tessa made plans on their own to go shopping at the mall. Luke was working at the clinic in the morning, but in the afternoon he'd called and asked Morgan to meet him for a late lunch, and of course they'd ended up at the houseboat.

Even the memory of their lovemaking caused an achy warmth in her abdomen. He brought out either the best or the worst in her, she hadn't made up her mind which. She only knew that Saturday had been wild and crazy and delicious.

He was a superb lover, generous and inventive. He'd spent time and care lavishly to bring her pleasure. And then, not wanting the enjoyment of being with him to end, she'd said, "I've got a great idea—let's pick up Chinese food and have dinner together at my house, all of us."

Luke had seemed to consider it, but then he shook his head. "I've got a patient I have to see at St. Joe's and some lab work to run. Then there's a woman coming this evening to apply for the housekeeper position, so Sophie needs to be home. Sorry, my love.''

Morgan was disappointed, but it wasn't until later that evening, when she and Tess and India were eating the Chinese food she'd ordered anyway, that she really started thinking about it.

Apart from that one impromptu dinner the night of India's arrival, there'd been no contact between their families except the occasional meetings the girls arranged on their own, and Morgan had the distinct feeling Luke would have prevented those if he could.

It bothered her. She'd started waking up in the night, thinking about it, which was a sure sign she'd better bring it out in the open and just ask him what the heck was going on. It was one thing to have a lovely hideaway like the houseboat. It was quite another to turn their relationship into something clandestine and furtive. She'd talk it out with him the next time they were together, she decided.

And right now, Sophie was waiting.

Morgan made her way to the door of the consulting room and smiled warmly at the girl slumped in the plastic chair.

''Hi, Sophie. Boy, it's a miserable day out there, huh?''

''Yeah.''

Morgan tried again. ''I can't believe next

month's Christmas. I haven't even started my shopping yet, have you?''

"Nope." It was obvious Sophie didn't want to chat, so Morgan flipped open her file. "Now, let's get these pesky questions answered and then I'll have a look at you, okay?''

Sophie nodded, biting her bottom lip. Morgan could see that the girl was nervous, and she figured it was probably about the physical examination. To put Sophie more at ease, Morgan carefully explained every single detail of the examination procedure, but it didn't seem to help. Sophie just nodded and fiddled with the pendant she wore, her discomfort evident. At last she blurted out, "Can I ask you something, Morgan?''

"Absolutely. Anything at all.''

Sophie was all but wringing her hands, and Morgan hoped she'd be able to set the girl's mind at rest. She met Sophie's anxious gaze and smiled reassuringly. "What? Take a deep breath and spill it out.''

Sophie was staring down at her lap, and she gave Morgan a quick look from under her bangs. "Are you having an affair with my dad? 'Cause Tessa says you are.''

Morgan was taken completely off guard. The question was totally unexpected, and for a moment she couldn't breathe, much less answer.

She felt like a child caught out in mischief. She felt embarrassed and self-conscious and annoyed with herself. Over the past couple of weeks, she'd known she ought to talk to Tessa about Luke, explain that they were spending time together, but there hadn't been an opportunity. Or so she'd pretended.

India's presence in the house complicated everything, no doubt about it. She was like a spoiled, selfish child, always demanding Morgan's attention, making it hard to have private conversations with Tess.

But when it came down to it, Morgan knew it was really her own shyness that had stopped her. It was one thing to discuss birth control and sex in general terms with Tessa. It was quite another to admit she was involved in an intimate way with Luke.

Now Morgan understood too late that she ought to have made an opportunity rather than wait for one. She should have overcome her own inhibitions and been up front with her foster daughter. How could she have forgotten that Tess was bright, observant and very wise to the ways of the world?

Well, Sophie had asked a forthright question, and in Morgan's opinion, it demanded a forthright answer. She drew in a painful breath and tried to steady her voice.

"Yes, Sophie, I am. I'm having an, um, relationship with your father. I—I care very much for him. We should have talked to both you and Tess about this. I can see now it was wrong of us not to."

"Hey, no problem." Sophie's voice was brittle. "It's your business, right? You're both grown-ups. It's not like it was with me and Jason. I mean we're just *kids*. When you're grown up you can do whatever you want, right?"

Sophie tried for nonchalance, but there was terrible anger and betrayal in her tone and her words. Her chin quivered. "So, are you guys in love or what?"

Morgan's heart ached for this girl. She reached over and tried to take Sophie's hand in her own, but Sophie jerked it away. A renegade tear rolled down her cheek, and she scrubbed at it with the back of her hand.

Morgan wondered in desperation how she could possibly explain the complexities of her relationship with Luke to a fifteen-year-old child, particularly when she didn't begin to understand them herself. The only thing she could be was totally honest, she reminded herself again, no matter how difficult that was. And, man, was it tough.

"I do love your father, Sophie." It was the first time Morgan had admitted it to anyone except herself. She dreaded the question she sensed would be next: "So, does my father love you?"

To Morgan's immense relief, it didn't come. Sophie said instead, "Are you gonna get married?"

Morgan could see the undisguised fear on Sophie's face, and her heart contracted with pity. Sophie had already lost so much. This must feel to her as if she were losing her father, too.

"We've never discussed it, but no, I'd say we're not."

It was physically painful to admit that, even though she'd known it from the beginning. "The truth is, we haven't made any sort of long-range plans at all. This is a very new thing for both of us."

Sophie's shoulders slumped with her visible relief. "You're just sorta having *sex*, then, right?" There was more than a trace of contempt in her voice, and it hurt.

Morgan swallowed the lump in her throat and nodded, struggling to keep her voice even. "That's part of it, but Luke and I are friends, too, Sophie. More than anything, I don't want you or Tess hurt in any way by our actions, and I know your dad doesn't, either. I plan to talk to Tessa about this, and you need to talk it over with your father, tell him honestly and truly how you feel. I know how much he loves you, that he'll respect your feelings and your needs.''

''Yeah, right.'' Sophie sounded both defiant and angry. ''That'd be the day. I can't talk to him about *anything*. I'm just a big disgrace as far as my dad's concerned, getting pregnant and everything.'' Her voice trembled. ''And this just proves how he thinks about stuff. It's fine for him to be with you, be friends and...and even go to bed with you, but not say a word to me about it. He thinks I'm some little kid or something. Even after my mom died, he never really *talked* to me about it.''

Tears were streaming down Sophie's cheeks now, and Morgan silently handed her a fistful of tissues, appalled at the way the girl saw her relationship with Luke.

''My dad isn't like you, Morgan, y'know? Tessa says you don't give her a hard time over stuff. Like when she's with Dylan, right? Tessa sees him whenever she wants and you don't get on her case about it, but my dad won't even let me talk to Jason, and he's...he's my baby's *father*.''

Sophie's pain was spilling out, her words laden with blame and hurt. ''Jason was *my* friend, I *love* him, but now he never phones me or sees me or anything, 'cause Daddy won't let him.''

Morgan doubted that. She knew enough about teenagers to know that if Jason wanted to be in touch, he'd find a way no matter how obstructive Luke chose to be.

It sounded as if Jason had taken the easy way out of a difficult situation, but of course Morgan didn't say that to Sophie. The girl was suffering, and without meaning to, Morgan had made things even more painful for her. She couldn't see how to help except to validate how Sophie was feeling, encourage her to talk and then just listen.

"It's been really tough for you, Sophie. I understand that. First losing your mom, then moving and now being pregnant. Boy, that's a lot to have happen to you when you're fifteen."

Sophie sniffled and nodded, her face a study in misery. "I hate my life. I just want everything to be the way it was before my mom died. It isn't fair."

"How was it before?" Luke never talked about his marriage.

"We were a family. Mummy and Daddy and me. Like, we had this great house in Victoria, and my mom was always there when I came home from school. And Daddy took us for dinner on Sunday, and she baked cookies and stuff, and her and my dad *really, really* loved each other, and—"

Morgan listened, and her heart felt as if it were breaking for this daughter of the man she loved. When Sophie ran out of steam, Morgan said in a soft tone, "Life isn't always fair, Soph. I remember feeling a lot like you do when I was your age." She explained briefly about India marrying one man after another and how lonely and scared that had made her feel, about moving constantly from one school to another as their circumstances changed.

Sophie paid attention, and Morgan could see that sharing her own experiences had comforted the girl. When she was calmer, Morgan gently examined her, encouraging her to talk about her baby, answering any questions Sophie asked and bringing up the ones Morgan knew were difficult for the girl to verbalize.

By the time the appointment was over and she was dressed again, Sophie obviously felt better. She shoved her hair back behind her ear and said in an embarrassed tone, "I'm sorry I said all that stuff about you and my dad."

"That's okay." Morgan felt as if she'd had surgery without an anesthetic, but she forced a reassuring smile. "Don't be sorry, Soph. It's always good to talk about the things that are bothering you."

"Yeah. I guess. Well, thanks, Morgan. See ya." The office door shut behind her, and Morgan closed her eyes and flopped back in her chair.

She had to talk to Tessa. If Sophie was this upset and angry and worried, it stood to reason Tessa would be, too. And something Sophie had said was niggling at Morgan.

Tessa can see Dylan whenever she wants.

Did that mean that Tess had started going out with him again? Because if she had, Morgan wasn't aware of it, just as she'd been unaware that Tess knew all about herself and Luke. How many other things were going on in the girl's life that Morgan didn't know about?

Even worse, when had they stopped confiding in each other?

A feeling of panic gripped her, and she reached for the phone. She wanted to talk to Luke. She knew he'd be at St. Joe's right now. He should be told how insecure Sophie was, and how unhappy, Morgan reasoned. She longed to discuss all the other things that were troubling her, as well—Tessa, Dylan, India. But before she'd finished dialing, Morgan broke the connection and slowly laid the phone down.

Sophie was her patient, she reminded herself. What the girl had just confided was confidential. More than that, Luke was making it plain by his actions that he didn't want involvement except on a sexual level. Maybe he didn't want her telling him her problems.

He'd said many times, in many ways, that he wanted her in his arms, in his bed. He hadn't said a word about involving her in the rest of his life or becoming involved in hers.

She'd have to find some way to help Sophie, though. And she needed to bridge the distance between herself and Tessa, fast. She also had to try to do something about the open antagonism between Tess and India.

If only India would pack up and go back to Florida where she belonged.

Feeling weary to the bone, Morgan got to her feet and made her way to the next examining room, where another patient had been waiting far too long for her attention.

She'd never felt less like dealing with patients, listening to their problems, calming their fears.

She'd never felt more like consulting an analyst about the mess her own life had suddenly become.

"YOU WERE RIGHT about Morgan and my dad."

Tessa's stomach felt suddenly sick. It was one thing to guess and another to know for certain. She watched Sophie plop a lump of butter into the bowl and add sugar, attacking the cookie mixture as though it were a mortal enemy.

It was Monday evening, and they'd decided to skip their meeting at the community center and come over to Sophie's place instead. Sophie's dad was out somewhere and wouldn't be back until much later, and they both agreed that shortbread would make them feel better than listening to the other girls in the group moaning about their problems.

"I had my appointment with Morgan this afternoon, so I just asked her. If, you know, they were doing it. And she said yeah."

"Well, no big surprise, right? Anybody could've guessed, the way they're both acting. They must figure we're blind or something." Tessa wasn't about to reveal how betrayed she felt by having Morgan admit something that intimate to Sophie and still not say a word to her.

"Yeah, I guess." Sophie added a cup of flour to the dough and Tessa smeared oil on a cookie sheet. "She says she loves my dad but they're not getting married."

"Yeah, right. Grown-ups never tell the truth about stuff like that. My last foster parents went on and on about how they'd never get divorced, and then they did." Tessa wished Sophie would just drop the subject. She didn't want to hear any more about it. She didn't want to think about what would happen to her if Morgan and Doc Gilbert decided to get married. She'd always had the feeling that even though he liked her, he didn't really approve of her.

It was different for Sophie—she was his real kid. He had to take care of her, no matter who he married. But Tessa knew all too well it was different when you were a foster kid.

"Here, Soph, let me do that. It says here to work it like pie dough, not beat the stuffing out of it." Tessa took the bowl from Sophie and began to knead the mixture with her fingers. "So, you gonna come over to the Hot Spot with me later? Dylan's meeting me there for a burger, and Brody'll be there. Dylan told me he thinks you're hot." Dylan and his friend Brody Rathbone had met Sophie at the mall on the weekend, when she and Tessa were shopping.

"Yeah, right. And guys really like girls with big stomachs. Give me a break."

"I told you before, you don't show hardly at all, 'specially with that loose top. It's real cute. And Brody doesn't know anything. Dylan, either. I didn't say a word to him about you having a baby."

Tessa rolled out the dough and handed Sophie one of the cookie cutters, a heart. "Seems to me you got a right to have some fun once in a while. And if Jason hears about it, so what? A little competition might do him a lotta good.'' But Tessa didn't feel all that wonderful about coaxing Sophie to come with her. Sophie was an innocent. She couldn't really take care of herself the way *she* could, Tessa concluded.

And she didn't much like Brody Rathbone, when it came down it. He might be Dylan's newest best buddy, but he was a bit of a sleazeball, in her opinion. Sophie's dad would freak right out if he ever found out Sophie was anywhere near somebody like Brody Rathbone. Tessa knew that would do it as far as she was concerned. He'd never let her near Sophie again.

Well, serve the doc right. Why should she worry about Sophie's dad? Tessa thought. He didn't think she was good enough to be Sophie's friend anyhow. And he sure wasn't home making supper right now, was he? She'd bet Morgan wasn't, either. They were probably off somewhere together, getting it on. The only person who was ever home these days seemed to be the old lady, and she was there all the time—she never stepped foot outside the door. Tessa had had about all she could take of India. She'd somehow even stolen Skippy away, and he was supposed to be Tessa's dog.

''So what d'ya say, Soph? Wanna come?''

Sophie hesitated and then nodded. ''Okay. I

guess. I've gotta be back before ten, though. My father said he'd be home about then.''

"No problem. I told Dylan I'd meet him at seven. We got lotsa time. Here, shove these on this cookie sheet and we'll put them in the oven. We can find a box and take the guys some— they'd get off on that.''

What the heck, she and Sophie deserved a little fun. And the hollow feeling in the pit of her gut was probably just because she was hungry.

CHAPTER FIFTEEN

TESSA WAS A LITTLE drunk, but she made certain Sophie didn't touch a drop.

Dylan and Brody had smuggled a bottle of vodka into the café, but no way was she gonna let Soph drink. Everybody with half a brain knew what alcohol did to a fetus.

Tess hadn't eaten much except a couple of the cookies they'd made, so the alcohol went straight to her head. She couldn't seem to stop laughing, and she knew she was acting goofy, but the guys were being a big bore, bragging it up about some new business they had and how they were gonna get rich.

Dylan pulled her close and showed her a roll of twenties. "You need anything, baby, you let old Dylan know. Soon as you're sixteen and legal, we can go travelin' down to California or Florida on the bike, right?"

Yeah, right. Weird, how she used to really believe Dylan when he talked like that. She'd really wanted to go with him once, but now she wasn't so sure.

She'd gotten this thing in her head about finishing school and maybe even going on to art
school afterward. Just last week her teacher had
said she had talent. He wanted her to enroll in a
special drawing class.

They made her nervous, all these new feelings, so she had another gulp of her drink and
then started pretending as if she were India to
make Sophie laugh, acting like she was some big
movie star or something, really camping it up.

But of course the guys didn't get it.

"India's Morgan's mother," she explained.
"She's, like, this really bummed-out old actress.
She used to live in Hollywood and do laundry-
soap commercials, but she acts like she was a
major movie star or something."

Tessa tilted her head back and half closed her
eyes, trying for a facsimile of India's deep, dramatic voice. "Bette Davis? But of course I knew
Betty, although she was rather a lot older than
me. Our eyes are similar, darling. And I married
her third cousin once removed. He gave me this
gold bracelet, or was it my diamond earrings?
No, no, it had to be the sterling collar."

Sophie giggled. "Or maybe it was that fur
coat you said she has."

"Yeah? What kinda fur coat?" Dylan, at
least, was showing some interest. Brody Rathbone was such a pig, he just slumped in the cor-

ner of the booth with his eyes half shut, staring at Sophie's boobs and salivating. Honestly.

"Oh, I dunno. Mink, probably."

"Tessa says her jewelry's all real, too. Right, Tess?" Sophie moved a little farther away from Brody.

"Oh, yeah, it's real all right." Even though India was a royal pain in the butt, Tess couldn't help but admire her belongings. She sneaked into India's room sometimes when the old woman was sleeping downstairs and tried things on.

"She told me she got it all as gifts from Hollywood studios and things, but I don't believe her. She's been married umpteen dozen times. I figure she took the guys for all she could get and then bought herself all that stuff with the money."

"Figures," Dylan sneered. "Broads are famous for that. So, is she really rich, this old bitch?" He snickered at his rhyme and poured more vodka into the soda glasses, but Tess didn't really want more. She was feeling dizzy and sort of sick. She also felt a little uneasy at making fun of India. She was Morgan's mother. It didn't really feel right to ridicule her.

"She's got her jewelry and clothes and stuff. I guess if she sold that she'd be rich, but she hasn't got much money." Tess had sneaked a peek at India's bankbooks one day when she left her purse in the bathroom.

All at once Tess was ashamed of herself for poking through India's things. And she was bored to death with Dylan and Brody and their bragging.

"C'mon, Soph, we better get going. You said your dad was gonna be home at ten and it's almost nine already." She grabbed her coat and handed Sophie hers.

"What's the big rush, Tess?" Dylan was annoyed. "Stick around. We ain't even had burgers yet. I can run you home on the bike later on."

"Sure, Tessa, you stay here. I can drive Sophie home—I got my car outside." Brody came to life for the first time all evening, reaching for his coat.

"Not," Tessa muttered under her breath. No way was she sending Soph anywhere alone with Brody Rathbone.

"No, thanks. We're both takin' the bus." She slipped her jacket on and waited for Sophie.

Dylan watched her, eyes narrowed with displeasure. "Be ready to go Thursday night around eight, Tessa. There's a party over at Pete's place. I'll come by on the bike for ya."

Pete was a real druggie.

"Sorry, Dylan. I'm goin' out that night." It

was the play at the church, the one she'd helped design the sets for. She'd thought briefly of asking Dylan to come and see it, but he'd make fun of her for having anything to do with a church, and she really didn't want him to even know.

"Oh, yeah? And just who're ya goin' out with?"

"With the whole football team, who d'ya think?" Tessa realized too late that she'd made Dylan mad, and she quickly changed her tone. "With Morgan and her mother. We're going to a play."

"A play, huh? Well, la de da. If that's how yer gonna be, screw you, Tessa. There's lotsa babes out there. You can go to hell. And take yer little friend with ya." With a vicious sweep of his arm, Dylan sent the glasses flying off the table.

Sophie let out a terrified squeal.

Tessa saw a waitress hurry into the back, and a man in a cook's apron came running out.

"Let's go." Tessa grabbed Sophie's arm and hustled them both out of the café, wondering as they ran hand in hand down the street to the bus stop why Dylan suddenly seemed like an even bigger jerk than Brody.

MORGAN SQUINTED at the watch she'd tossed on the bedside table and yawned. She had to get up, but the warmth of Luke's body and the way his arms cradled her made her settle again, conscious of the seconds ticking by, but reluctant to move. They were curled spoon fashion, her back to his front, and it felt like heaven.

Ten more minutes, she promised herself. Ten more minutes, and then she'd go for sure.

"You awake, love?" His breath tickled the hair on her neck, and she wriggled onto her back and turned her head to look at him. He kissed her nose and she smiled at him, her heart contracting with love. His hair was mussed and his eyes had the heavy, contented look they got after lovemaking.

"You dozed off. I could feel the difference in your breathing," he said. "You're tired. I wish we could just stay here the rest of the night." His voice deepened. "I'd like to wake up beside you here some morning soon."

"Me, too, Luke." She'd like to wake up beside him in her own bed, so very much, but wanting that was dangerous.

"What time is it?"

"Eight forty-five."

"Damn. I have to go. I told Sophie I'd be home at ten," he said, reluctance evident in his tone. "I wish to God she'd settle on a housekeeper. She's found some reason to reject every single person who's answered my ad."

Morgan thought of the way Sophie's face had looked that afternoon when she spoke of Luke, the longing and the resentment intermingled. "Maybe she just wants you all to herself for a while," she said cautiously. "Sophie's probably feeling scared. She's bound to be really vulnerable and insecure right now. She needs her daddy."

It was as close as Morgan dared come to bringing up the violent emotions she knew Sophie harbored.

He cocked an eyebrow at her, his green eyes too perceptive. "She told you that when she came in for her checkup today?"

Morgan avoided his eyes. "Not in so many words," she lied. "It's just obvious to me she feels that way." She moved away from him and swung her legs over the edge of the bed.

"Where did you pitch my underwear?" She got down on her hands and knees, peering under the bed as her mind flitted over the things that were troubling her.

"I'm going to talk to Tessa about us, Luke. Maybe you ought to do the same with Sophie."

Morgan found her panties and got to her feet, stepping into them. "I'm really worried about Tess. This thing with her and India is making me crazy. It's mostly India's fault," she confided, forgetting that she'd decided not to tell him her problems. "She won't quit ordering Tess around, expecting her to wait on her hand and foot. I've talked to her, for all the good it does. It's an awful thing to say, but I wish the holidays were over so she'd go home. Honestly, I could wring her neck sometimes."

She glanced up and realized that Luke wasn't listening to a thing she was saying. He was looking at her as if she'd taken leave of her senses.

"What did you mean when you said I should talk to Sophie about us? You can't possibly believe I should tell my daughter that you and I are lovers?"

He sounded so aghast that Morgan would have laughed if the situation wasn't so serious.

She tossed the blankets aside, found her bra near the bottom of the bed and put it on. Her tights were on top of the dresser, and she sat down on the bed and struggled into them.

"You won't have to tell her, Luke. She already knows." She gave her skirt a shake and stepped into it. It was pretty badly creased, but what the heck. She was only going home.

"You *told* her? About us?" He was aghast.

Morgan shrugged and smiled at him, buttoning her blouse and tucking it in. "She asked me, so, yeah, I did. But she already knew. Tessa told her. They're very bright young women, Luke. They can put two and two together."

"I happen to think my sex life is my own private business, Morgan, not something to be discussed with fifteen-year-old children." He was shoving his legs into his trousers, and it was obvious by the ferocity of his actions that he was angry with her.

Damn the man! How could he be so smart and yet so blind to things he needed to see? There was so much going on with Sophie that he ought to realize and didn't, but he was all steamed up because the kid knew about sex, for Pete's sake. How did he figure she'd gotten pregnant?

Granted, there was plenty going on with Tess, too, but Morgan was going to get to the bottom of that right away, she vowed. At least she was aware there was something wrong.

Morgan knew she probably shouldn't interfere in his relationship with his daughter, but she thought of Sophie's face, the anger and pain reflected there, and she threw caution to the winds. Somebody had to tell him.

"Sophie's not a child, Luke. Unfortunately, she's not an adult, either. She's caught somewhere between and she's about to have a baby. She needs all the support she can get right now—from you and everyone around her." Well, she'd blown it already, she might as well dump the rest on him.

"Most of all, I think she needs to be in touch

with her baby's father. I think you're making a huge mistake keeping them apart. You ought to let them deal with this together."

There, it was out. She steeled herself for the inevitable explosion.

Luke had shrugged into his shirt, and he was sitting on the bed pulling on his socks. There was a long, tense moment of strained silence, and then he said in a dangerously quiet tone, "Do you, Morgan? Well, I think you make a huge mistake letting Tessa run wild with that thug who fathered her baby, so we're even. We don't agree on child-rearing methods and it's probably best that we don't discuss them."

His controlled, superior tone infuriated her, and his criticism hurt, because Dylan was an issue that she'd spent half the afternoon worrying about.

Her voice rose. "That's how you deal with issues, is it, by not discussing them? Ignoring things doesn't make them go away, you know. I'd have thought you'd have learned that by now, because Sophie sure isn't a happy young woman. And I feel sorry for her, because I see how hard it is to talk anything over with you."

This time she succeeded in making him lose control. He'd been trying to knot his tie, and he ripped it off and rounded on her. "Damn you,

Morgan! Why must you meddle in things that aren't your concern?''

Here it was, the thing she knew was between them, would always be between them, the thing that hurt her more than anything else. He wanted her, but only in part of his life, this sexual, passionate part they did so well together, but not in any other. He wanted a mistress instead of a partner. He wanted a lover instead of a friend.

"Sophie's my patient, Luke. She's become my concern whether you like it or not. Oh, I know you'd be more comfortable if she and I had never met. I know that very well.'' Her voice rose with her temper, and words came out that she'd never planned to say to him, at least not now.

"This houseboat of yours. It's like…like a little island to you, isn't it? A place to make love to me, to hide away, to keep this part of your life separate from the rest? Well, it doesn't work that way with me. I spill over, don't I, Luke? And that bothers you. As you just said, I meddle.''

"Don't be ridiculous.''

He was every bit as angry as she was, and that satisfied her. It was about time he got emotionally involved. Some small part of her realized she was out of control, but the rest of her didn't care. She'd been lying to herself and to him, and it was time for honesty.

"There's nothing ridiculous about any of this. The only ridiculous thing is that I love you, you stupid man, and you don't even see it!" she shouted at him. It felt terrifying and liberating to holler this way. "I want to be included in your life, *all* of your life, not just the bits you feel are suitable. I want marriage and children and all the problems that go with them, not a few hours every couple of days on a houseboat. And if you won't offer me all that, I'll find someone who will." The words were out before she could stop them, and once they were, she felt incredible relief.

He stared at her, openmouthed, shocked out of his anger.

"I love you," she repeated with passion, her voice still decibels louder than normal. "I care what happens to you. I care what happens to Sophie and her baby and the young man she loves. I also know that's the last thing you want, me and my messy feelings slopping all over your tidy life." She was shaking, and she couldn't for the life of her remember where she'd left her boots. She stormed out of the bedroom, aware that he was behind her.

"Morgan, wait just a minute here. We need

to talk. You can't just say these things and then leave."

"Why not? There's nothing much left to talk about." One of her boots was on the kitchen counter. The other had landed in the sink. How in heck had it gotten there? She grabbed them and shoved her feet into them, then rescued her coat from the floor by the door and put it on.

"I can't do this anymore. I guess I've found out I'm an all-or-nothing kind of person. I can't go on not wanting anything from you except what we have here."

She opened the door and gasped at the force of the wind and rain. "I want it all. I want you and Sophie over for Christmas dinner, I want to spoil her baby rotten when it comes, I want you to fight with India for me, I want to go to bed with you and not have to get up like this and go home afterward." She stepped out on the deck and turned to look at him. His shirttails were hanging out, his feet bare. He looked so beautiful it hurt her heart.

"And, Luke, I really do think you ought to at least let Sophie talk to her baby's father, because she's really unhappy about the way you've handled that. 'Bye."

"Morgan, you come back here."

She ignored him. She hurried down the gangplank and along the walkway.

BY THE TIME Luke got his shoes on and made it out to the parking lot, her Jeep was gone.

Bloody, bloody *hell*. Fuming with anger and frustration, he unlocked his car and climbed inside, slamming the door after himself hard enough to damage it.

He didn't start the motor, however. Instead, he sat and stared blindly out at the downpour, trying to figure out how a simple disagreement had escalated into Morgan's leaving him.

She'd begun by saying Sophie was unhappy. Well, that was nothing new. He knew all too well Sophie was unhappy, and having Morgan remind him felt like a knife twisting in his chest.

Talk to her, Morgan had insisted, and he would, God, he would, if only he knew what to say to reach the girl. He'd tried and failed time after time these past weeks, and just when he thought he was making headway, everything fell apart again.

He'd made so many mistakes with Sophie, maybe there wasn't any hope for the two of them. He remembered his own distant relationship with his mother and shuddered. He wanted so much more than that with his own daughter.

He'd tried to figure out where he'd gone wrong, and he understood some of it. When Sophie was little, he'd been focused on his career, aware that Deborah expected a certain life-style.

Her parents had money, and his didn't anymore, and it was a sore point between them. He'd been determined to provide his wife with all the things she seemed to want, so he'd worked instead of taking time to get to know his daughter; consequently Deborah had been the one Sophie grew close to.

And then, after Deborah's death, his sense of betrayal had been so great he'd again ignored the child, allowing his work to consume both his time and his energy, using it to dull the pain and anger, too self-centered to see what he was doing to Sophie.

He scrubbed at his face with his palm, pretending the moisture there was rain.

He didn't want to remember the other things Morgan had said, but he couldn't avoid them.

She loved him. She'd shouted that she loved him, and he'd felt the words in his gut, like a punch he hadn't been expecting.

He told himself he didn't want her love, didn't want the responsibility of it. He slammed his fist on the steering wheel and reminded himself that, after all, love was easy for Morgan. How many times had he heard her say she loved every baby she delivered? According to her, she loved the majority of her patients, more than a few nurses and her animal menagerie. She loved Tessa, sunny days, rainy days, bagels and chocolate cake. She loved snow, her house, rain, and she'd even said she loved one of the elderly maintenance men at St. Joe's.

So it shouldn't drive him totally mad to have her include him on her endless list, should it? It did, though, and he knew exactly why.

He loved her, too, and he felt as if he'd die if he lost her. He slumped down in the seat and closed his eyes. He didn't want to love her. In fact, he'd tried not to.

Damn it, he'd *really* tried. She was an exasperating, infuriating, meddling woman. She didn't fit any pattern he'd ever encountered, she didn't play by polite rules, she was an unpredictable witch in bed and she was more honest than anyone had any right to be.

She was a narcotic he couldn't give up, but she'd just given up on him.

A bitter smile tilted his mouth. She'd said it herself. Try as he would to contain her, Morgan spilled over, infiltrating every area of his life, shining her light into every hidden corner of his heart and soul.

He had to get her back. He had to figure out a way to mend himself and his life so it was suitable for Morgan to share. He had a hunch that meant admitting he'd been wrong, not just about Sophie, but about Adam Hendricks and

Jason. It would be the hardest thing he'd ever done.

He started the car, wishing he was a drinking man.

CHAPTER SIXTEEN

LUKE DIDN'T SLEEP much that night. He was up and dressed before six, and just before six-thirty he knocked on the Hendrickses' back door. Adam was an early riser.

Luke had spent half the night trying to figure out what to say, but when Adam opened the door, all the speeches he'd prepared went straight out of his head.

"Morning, Luke," Adam said in a neutral voice. "What can I do for you?"

Their last meeting had been ugly, and Luke knew he was to blame. He came right out with it. "I owe you an apology, Adam. I'm sorry for the way I've acted."

"Come on in and have a cup of coffee," Adam said, his craggy face solemn.

Luke sat at the cluttered table, and Adam poured two mugs full of coffee from an oversize pot and sat across from him, offering Luke the sugar bowl. "Sophie didn't agree to an abortion?"

"No, or adoption, either. She's determined to keep her baby and raise it herself."

Adam nodded. "She's a good, brave girl. That takes a lot of courage."

Sophie *was* brave. Luke felt an unexpected surge of pride in his daughter. "I've fired Eileen, and we're looking for a housekeeper who likes kids."

"Smart move. Eileen always made me feel as if I had rabies or something." Adam grinned, and Luke began to relax a little.

"When the baby comes, I'll help her all I can, of course, but I'm better at delivering than diapering." Luke shook his head. "I don't feel ancient enough to be a grandfather."

Adam smiled. "Me, either, but I'm sure we'll get the hang of it." He lifted his mug and took a drink. He was waiting, and Luke knew it. He took a deep breath and forced himself to add, "I've changed my mind about Jason, Adam. She needs him. I see that now." It wasn't easy to say; he still harbored dark thoughts about Jason.

Adam nodded emphatically. "Damned right she needs him. I've felt that all along. He's the baby's father, and I've wanted him to take responsibility, but you were the one who said no contact with Sophie." There was still a trace of resentment in his tone, and Luke understood.

Adam loved Jason the same way he loved Sophie.

"Yes, I know. I'm sorry."

Adam blew out a huge sigh. "This is one hell of a big relief to me, Luke. Peggy'll be really happy about this."

The words almost choked him, but Luke forced himself to say, "Tell Jason I'd be pleased if he'd get in touch with her as soon as possible."

"I'll do that. And it goes without saying that Peggy and I will be right there for the two of them and the baby. Those kids of ours need to finish their schooling, and they're gonna need a lotta help from all of us."

Luke finished his coffee and rose to his feet. "I should go." He paused when he reached the door. "This has been a tough test of a friendship, Adam, but I'd like to think we can salvage something of ours."

"So do I." Adam held out a hand, and Luke shook it hard.

Back at the house, he'd barely walked in the door when the phone rang. Luke answered, and after a few very polite and stilted sentences, he climbed the stairs, opened the door to Sophie's room and gently shook her awake.

Groggy, she sat up and rubbed her eyes, puzzled when Luke handed her the phone. His reward for one of the most difficult mornings of his life was the expression on her face when he said, "Jason's on the line. He wants to talk to you."

ODDLY ENOUGH, for the first time in Morgan's life, India actually noticed there was something wrong with her.

"You've lost your color, dear," she said, scrutinizing Morgan closely. "Would you like to use some of my blush?"

It was Thursday evening, and Morgan was ready to leave for the concert, waiting in the downstairs hall for Tessa. India had declared at dinner that she couldn't bear watching amateurs on a stage making fools of themselves and that she wouldn't be going.

"Is there some problem at work, Morgan?"

Morgan shook her head, too filled with anguish to even bother hiding it. "I've been seeing Luke, and we had a fight."

"The course of true love never runs smooth," India intoned in a mellifluous voice, glancing at the watch on her wrist. "Where is that girl? You'd think if you can get home early and be ready on time, she could at least make the effort. No consideration, these young people." She made her way into the living room and lowered herself to the sofa with a sigh. "Come and sit down and tell me what the fight was about. Goodness knows I've had enough experience with men to be able to give good advice on how to handle them.''

Considering her mother's spectacular divorce record, that statement would have been hilarious if Morgan hadn't felt so wretched. She sat down in the armchair, wishing she could just stay home like India, but of course she couldn't. Tessa had been talking about the set for weeks now, and although Morgan had been just as excited about seeing it, all her enthusiasm and pleasure in things large and small seemed to have gone out of her life in the past three days.

All she could think of was Luke. She didn't regret the things she'd said to him, but once the anger had gone, there was an awful emptiness inside her, a frightening sense of anguish and of loss.

''Let's get a move on, Morgan. We're gonna be late,'' Tessa called from the bottom of the stairs. Her voice was sulky, and as Morgan followed the girl out the back door she realized that Tessa wasn't in any better humor than she was. Maybe they should all just stay home and go to bed.

The little neighborhood church Morgan attended was filled with smiling faces, and the set Tessa had helped design was truly inspired. The actors did their best to bring their characters to life, and Morgan tried her best to capture the spirit of the occasion, but secretly it was a relief when the final curtain came down.

Morgan clapped and then turned to Tessa, forcing enthusiasm into her voice. "Your set was spectacular, Tess. You can be really proud of yourself. You did a fantastic job."

"Yeah, whatever," Tessa said with a sneer. She gave a world-weary shrug and got to her feet, pulling on her jacket and not waiting for Morgan as she made her way into the crowd that surged down the aisle toward the exit.

Morgan felt her face flame, and for a split second, she felt like bursting into tears. Tessa had been outright rude all evening, and this was the final straw. She put on her own coat and made her way out of the church into the unrelenting rain, responding with a strained smile to the countless cheery greetings that came her way.

Tessa was waiting by the Jeep. Morgan unlocked the doors, got in and started the motor. Tessa sat with her arms folded across her chest, chewing gum and staring out the side window.

Morgan made an effort to control herself. "That wasn't very nice, Tessa, walking away from me like that without a word. Why are you acting this way?"

Tessa shrugged and didn't answer.

"I thought we agreed a long time ago that we'd talk over whatever was bothering us."

"I'm gonna tell Frannie I need to live someplace else." Tessa's voice was hard and distant.

Morgan felt as if she'd been slapped across the face. This was preposterous! It couldn't be happening! "Live someplace else?" She wheeled the Jeep to the curb and jerked to a stop. "You want to move out? I don't believe you're saying this. Tessa, what on earth is this all about? Talk to me, please."

Tessa stared straight ahead and chewed her gum.

"Is it India? Oh, Tessa, I know you don't get along with her—I don't get along with her very well, either. But she'll be leaving right after the New Year...."

"No, she won't." Tess turned burning, angry eyes on Morgan. "She told me today she's staying. Forever. The rest of her life. She's moved in with us...with you, only she didn't bother to tell you.

"Today she was ordering me around, like she always does, and I said something about her going home. She said if anybody left, it would be me. You were her daughter, and she was gonna live with you the rest of her life."

Morgan was speechless. She gaped at Tess,

totally at a loss for words. "That...that can't be right. She's just goading you," she finally spluttered. "She has this big trailer in Florida...."

"No, she doesn't. She sold it. That's why she's got so much stuff with her. She's moved here, don't you see? And if she's gonna stay, I'm not. I know she's your mother, but I can't stand her, Morgan. Besides, nothin's the same anymore. You're never around—you don't really care about me now."

"Tess, that's not true. I love you. Surely you know that."

"No, you don't. You love Sophie's father. You even told her about it, but you never said a word to me."

With a sinking heart, Morgan realized how many things she'd overlooked during the past weeks. Tess had needed her and she'd been preoccupied. With Luke.

Quietly, she did her best to explain their relationship, just as she'd done earlier with Sophie. "It's over now—it wasn't working," she finished, and the words brought such unbearable pain she could hardly stand it. "And I'm sorry for hurting you. I never meant that to happen."

Morgan's fingers trembled as she reached to turn on the ignition. "As for the situation with India, I think we'd better go home right now and have a talk, all three of us."

IT TOOK ENORMOUS EFFORT, but when Morgan and Tessa finally left, India went into the bathroom and began the skin-care regimen she'd performed all her life. She rubbed the rich cleansing cream slowly over her face, trying to ignore the fact that her facial bones were becoming more and more prominent as the disease worsened. She seemed to have lost quite a lot of weight over the past two weeks, although her belly had swollen.

Skippy lay on the bath mat watching her with his wise brown eyes. Wasn't it strange how fond she'd become of this little deaf dog? Morgan and Tessa were out so much of the time, he'd become like a close friend.

"I'm tired tonight, Skippy. Arguing with that brat of a girl takes it out of me. I don't know how I'll ever make it up those cursed stairs to go to bed."

How fortunate the house had this roomy bathroom on the main floor. She'd worked out a system so she only had to go upstairs once a day, at bedtime, but it meant sending Tessa up for anything she'd forgotten. And the girl could be downright mean and really ornery about it, India thought with a touch of admiration. She'd do fine in the world, would Tessa.

And *she'd* soon be out of it, India thought sadly. If that doctor in Florida was right, this would be her last holiday season. In years past, she'd always gone to glittery parties all during December.

She shook her head at the caricature in the mirror. Tonight she hadn't even been able to make it to a small church to watch some awful amateur acting. Being ill and old was disgusting. And she was going to have to tell Morgan about her heart. Tessa would surely spill the beans about the trailer, and then Morgan would know this was more than just a visit.

She damped down the fear that never quite went away these days. She and Morgan didn't get on any better than they ever had, it was true, but blood was thicker than water. Morgan would take care of her, India assured herself. And fooling Morgan this long made her feel quite smug.

"Not even smart doctors know everything, Skippy."

It somehow made the silly disease less real, less powerful, if India's clever daughter could live with her and not detect it.

Panting and trying to ignore the irregular hammering of her heart, she used a tissue to remove the cream and then had to sit on the closed toilet seat for what seemed a long time before she could walk down the hall to the living room.

Skippy trotted along behind her, his nails making clicking noises on the wooden floor. India was wearing her warm velour dressing gown, and she looked at the stairs and then lowered herself to the sofa in front of the fire for just a few moments. She'd go up to bed a little later. For now, it was warm and cozy here. She'd rest before she climbed those dratted stairs. She lifted her feet up with difficulty and arranged the cushions behind her head so she could breathe easier. She closed her eyes.

Skippy lay down on the rug beside her, and she let her hand dangle down to stroke his fur. In a moment, she fell deeply asleep.

She awakened with a start, aware that Major had been barking outside and that Skippy was no longer beside her. India heard his toenails clicking as he ran up the stairs.

There was a loud noise up there and she jumped, heart pounding. She waited, thinking Morgan and Tessa were home, but then she heard Skippy yowling a high and frantic sound, as if he were in pain.

Concerned, India struggled to her feet, drew her dressing gown around her and then made her slow way along the hall to the bottom of the stairs. Skippy's cries went on and on, seeming to come from her bedroom.

Laboriously, she began the long climb, her heart thundering in her chest. Clinging to the banister, she was almost at the landing when she saw the two male figures hurrying down the stairs toward her. One of them carried a bulging black plastic garbage bag.

"That damned dog bit me," one of them was complaining in a loud voice. They saw her at the same moment she saw them, and they came to an abrupt stop. One of them let out a stream of curses.

"Thought nobody was gonna be home..."

With a birdlike squawk of terror, India turned and tried to run, knowing they were right behind her. She made it almost to the bottom of the stairs, but then her chest was on fire and her breath was gone, and in a show of bravado, she whirled around to face them. They were directly behind her, and when she suddenly stopped, one of them collided with her—hard. She lost her balance and tumbled backward. She was aware for an instant of falling through space, and then lights exploded in her skull just before the world went dark.

MORGAN WAS AS familiar with St. Joe's Emerg as she was with her own living room. She'd done her rotation down here during her internship, her friend Alex had worked here for years and Morgan herself often treated patients here, but tonight she was seeing it from a different perspective.

A few moments before, the ambulance carrying India had screamed into one of the bays, and Morgan had turned her unconscious mother over to the efficient Emerg staff.

Ambulance attendants rattled off neuro vitals—blood pressure, heart rate, respiration—while Morgan did her best to answer the questions fired at her, aware that what she could tell them was of little help. They transferred India from the ambulance stretcher as Morgan talked, aware that her voice was shaking.

"She was home alone and someone broke into the house. She either fell or was pushed down the stairs. No, she hasn't regained consciousness. No, I don't know how long she was unconscious, but we found her exactly twenty-three minutes ago. The only injury I could detect was that laceration on the back of her head. She's sixty-four, no allergies that I know of. No, there won't be any medical data on file, because she's visiting from Florida."

She knew the rules about relatives and kept out of the team's way, grateful that they let her stay, watching them remove India's dressing gown and nightie. Morgan gasped aloud when her mother's naked body was revealed under the harsh lights.

Except for her protruding belly, India was emaciated. Her arms and legs were skeletal, her once full breasts shrunken and flat against the bony wall of her chest.

Morgan hadn't seen her mother naked for many years, and shock rippled through every nerve ending as the team checked with meticulous care for further injuries.

"She...she's so thin," Morgan blurted out in a horrified tone, but no one heard her. The organized chaos was carefully orchestrated, and ER supervisor Dr. Greg Brulotte was very much in charge. Morgan knew Greg and respected him. He was excellent at his job, competent and caring.

"I want a full workup, blood tests, cardiogram and CT scan," he was saying as another team member reported, "Left pupil considerably larger than the right. Reflexes better on right side than left..."

Morgan barely heard them. She stared at India, who looked as fragile as old glass, the cords on her neck standing out like ropes against the diminished flesh. It struck her like a physical blow that this withered, frail body had once carried her inside it.

Her mother had always been strong, controlling, invincible. It had never crossed Morgan's mind that she could get old and sick. Morgan thought of how much she'd resented her coming to stay, how she'd disliked having India living in her home. Over the past weeks she'd wished fervently for her mother's departure, and tonight, when Tessa had said India was planning on staying, Morgan had been appalled at the thought.

She'd never once suspected that this pitiful skeletal body was hidden beneath India's elegant clothing and commanding personality.

What illness was she hiding? Morgan knew beyond a doubt that there was something seriously wrong with her mother, something far more than a concussion, and she felt mortified to think that she had lived with India and hadn't even noticed.

She hadn't asked about her health, and India hadn't told her. As much as she was able, she'd avoided conversations with her mother. And she was supposedly a doctor whose great gift was communicating.

She bowed her head and a deep sense of shame overwhelmed her.

CHAPTER SEVENTEEN

"THE CT SCAN REVEALS that your mother has a sizable subdural hematoma with considerable internal bleeding," Dr. Brulotte said to Morgan. "I gave her dexamethasone to reduce the swelling, and she should be waking up any moment now. Her heart rate is causing some concern, so I've ordered a chest X-ray. She's experiencing shortness of breath, and her blood pressure's dropping. Maybe when she regains consciousness she can tell us what the problem is."

The moment the portable X-ray machine was wheeled away, Morgan moved closer to the gurney where her mother lay. She took India's hand in hers, careful not to disturb the needle in her vein, and when her mother's eyelids fluttered open, Morgan smiled at her reassuringly.

"Tell me your name, honey. Do you remember your name?" One of the nurses began the usual questions to determine India's mental state, and after several seconds, India answered, but her gaze was vacant and panicked. It was several moments before she focused on her daughter's face.

"Mor-Morgan. Where…am I?" It was obviously difficult for her to speak.

"You've had an accident, India. You're in the hospital. We're taking good care of you."

"No…accident." India became agitated, struggling to sit up, and the nurses helped Morgan calm her.

"I…was sleeping, by…the fire," India explained. "Skippy was hurt. I…went to see. They…hurt Skippy." Her tone was indignant.

Morgan swallowed hard, and tried to smile encouragement over the lump in her throat when she thought of the little dog. Tessa had carried him downstairs. Morgan thought he'd broken either a leg or a hip, but she'd been too busy with India to examine him thoroughly. Morgan had given the dog a shot to ease his pain and told Tessa to call a cab and take him to the animal hospital.

"Two…men. Boys," India said, every word an effort. "Ran…down the stairs…knocked me…down. What…about…Skippy?"

Morgan struggled for control, aware that her voice was trembling. "I'm sure he's gonna be fine. Tess took him to the vet. What did these boys look like, Mother?"

India tried to shake her head and moaned.

"Short hair, tall…dark. Oh, I…don't know. So frightened…poor little dog." Tears streamed down her cheeks, and Morgan wiped them away.

"Mother, can you tell us what's wrong with you? You've got a concussion, but there's something more the matter, isn't there? We need to know what it is in order to treat you properly."

"Cardio…myopathy." The complicated word sighed off India's tongue with the ease of long familiarity, although her voice was barely above a whisper. "Had it…three years."

Morgan looked across at Dr. Brulotte, now studying the X rays that had just been handed to him. She knew her own face reflected the concern on his. He motioned toward the curtain surrounding the cubicle, and Morgan followed him outside.

"Cardiomyopathy." He shook his head, his frustration and tension evident. "It's unfortunate we didn't know sooner," he said in a low tone. "As you know, Doctor, dexamethasone unfortunately puts an extra strain on the heart, and the X rays show it's already considerably enlarged. I've put in a call for the heart specialist, but it's taking a while to locate him. Right now I'll load her up on cardiac meds and we'll just hope for—"

"Dr. Brulotte." The urgent note in the nurse's voice brought both doctors hurrying back into the cubicle, where it was immediately evident that India was in trouble. Her breathing was stertorous and she was losing consciousness again.

"Blood pressure's dropping, and she's cyanotic with an oxygen saturation of eighty-two percent."

"Up the oxygen to six liters and give digoxin, point five milligrams," Brulotte ordered, and as the nurses hurried to administer the medication that would hopefully stimulate India's heart, Morgan understood with sudden shocking clarity that her mother's chances of survival were slim.

"Morgan, there's a policeman who'd like to speak to you." Leslie Yates, the triage nurse, touched Morgan's shoulder.

There was nothing she could do for India. Feeling dazed, Morgan made her way out and over to the tall uniformed policeman waiting by the nursing station.

"Sorry to bother you, Doctor, but I'm Constable Graves," he began. "My partner and I responded to the 911 call at your residence. You were busy with your mother at the time, so you maybe don't remember me. How's your mother doing?"

"Not well." Morgan tried for a deep breath, but her lungs felt heavy. "She regained consciousness and said that she'd fallen asleep in front of the fireplace—she often does that."

Rapidly, Morgan related what India had told her. "These men who were in my house, I don't suppose you've caught them?"

He shook his head. "Not yet, but we'd like nothing better. We've had a number of similar break-ins in the past few months. This one was a little different, though."

He gave Morgan a long, appraising look. "There was no sign of forced entry. We talked to your daughter, and she says as far as she can tell the only room that was ransacked was your mother's. It appears your mother's jewelry and two fur coats were stolen from her room, as well as the wallet from her handbag. They didn't bother with the microwave or the television or the VCR. The fact that they went straight upstairs to your mother's room seems to indicate they knew exactly what they were after. Your bedroom and your daughter's room weren't disturbed at all. Do you know if the entrance doors were all locked?"

Morgan thought it over and nodded. "The front door is always locked, and I remember locking the back when Tessa and I left the house. I don't think my mother would have opened them again. The basement door has an iron bar across the inside."

"Do you hide a key anywhere outside?"

"Under a paving stone in the backyard." In

the summer, she and Tessa had once locked themselves out, and they'd hidden a key there. Morgan frowned. "So, you think this is someone who knows us? Who might know about the key?"

"It would certainly explain how they gained entry. We'll check on it. Is there anyone you know, or perhaps someone your daughter knows, who you think might be capable of this?"

A cold shudder ran through her as Morgan instantly thought of Dylan. "Did...did you talk to Tessa?"

He nodded. "We did. She insists she doesn't know anyone who'd break into your home." He was studying Morgan intently, and she looked away. "I'd appreciate any help you could give us on this matter, Dr. Jacobsen. I understand Tessa is a foster child who hasn't been with you that long?"

Morgan looked straight into his eyes. "Tessa's my daughter. I'm afraid I can't help you, Constable."

She really had nothing but her suspicions to go on, and she'd be betraying Tessa by not speaking to her first, Morgan assured herself, but she could feel the beginnings of outrage stirring inside her.

She remembered how Dylan had threatened her that day in the pool hall. And he'd struck

Tessa and caused her miscarriage. He was capable of this, Morgan was sure of it.

"If anything comes to mind, call this number." The constable handed her a card, and Morgan stuck it in her pocket without looking at it.
She stood frozen as he turned and walked away.
When he'd gone through the doors leading out
of the ER, Morgan hurried to the small staff
lounge.

It was empty, and she was grateful. She dialed
home and waited as the phone rang. Tessa was
obviously still at the animal hospital with Skippy.

Morgan's own voice came on the line as the
answering machine picked up, and she waited
impatiently and then, in a harsh tone she barely
recognized, said, "Tessa, I'm at St. Joe's. Call
me the moment you get in. I need to talk to
you."

She hung up, blood pounding in her ears, and
had to keep swallowing as she thought of her
mother, knocked down like a rag doll, and of
Skippy, broken and crying piteously. This
wasn't the time to be accusing or angry, she told
herself over and over.

But she couldn't control the fury that swept
through her like a hot, dry wind.

FORTY MINUTES LATER, her pager signaled that
Tessa was calling back, and Morgan hurried to

the phone.

"Tess, how's Skippy?" Morgan controlled her voice with difficulty.

"His hip is broken. They had to operate on him, but the vet thinks he'll be okay. They kept him there. The vet says it looks as if somebody with heavy boots might have kick—" Tessa's voice faltered. "Might have kicked him."

"And how're you?"

"Umm, okay, I guess. How's India?" Tessa sounded scared and miserable, like a little girl, and Morgan squeezed her eyes shut against the rush of conflicting emotions that raced through her. She felt sorry for Tessa, but she also felt compelled to tell the girl her suspicions about Dylan.

"India's not too good. She's…" Morgan's voice faltered. "She has a serious heart condition we didn't know about."

A choked sob from Tessa made Morgan realize that the girl was crying. She couldn't think what to say to comfort her.

"I'm probably going to be here the rest of the night, and I don't like you being in the house alone." She tried her best to sound casual. "I talked to the policeman who was at the house earlier. He thinks whoever did this might have used a key to get in—maybe that key we hid in the backyard.''

Morgan could hear Tessa's sharply indrawn breath, and she knew Tess understood perfectly what she was getting at.

"I'm pretty sure whoever did it won't come back, but I'd feel better if you weren't there alone," Morgan repeated. "Do you want to come down here and be with me?''

There was a long, strained silence.

"I'd rather stay with Sophie. She won't mind.''

Morgan hesitated, knowing how Luke might feel about that, but she was too emotionally drained to worry about it right now.

"Okay.'' She couldn't find the strength to say any more, to directly bring up the issue of Dylan, even though it was foremost in her mind. She knew she sounded aloof, but she couldn't help it. "Do you want me to call Luke and ask if he'll come and get you?''

"I'll call right now. And, Morgan?'' Tessa's voice was suddenly choked with sobs. "Oh, Morgan, I'm sorry.''

Morgan simply didn't have the energy to ask what Tess was sorry for. Part of her was too afraid of what the answer would be, and the intercom provided her with an excuse.

"Dr. Jacobsen to Emergency. Dr. Jacobsen to

Emergency." The soft female voice was calm, but panic built inside of Morgan as the message was repeated.

"Tess, we'll talk about this later. I've got to go now, they're paging me."

Morgan shoved the phone back in its cradle and ran for the door to Emerg.

LUKE WAS IN THE basement when the phone rang, trying to settle the Alsatian puppy he'd bought late that afternoon as a surprise for Sophie. He glanced at his watch. It was well past midnight. He picked up the extension, selfishly hoping no one had decided to have a baby tonight.

"Doc Gilbert? Hi, it's Tessa."

"Tessa, what is it?" He knew the instant he heard her strained voice that something was seriously wrong, and his fingers tightened around the receiver. *Morgan...*

"Our house got broken into tonight, and India's in the hospital." She told him the details, adding, "Who—whoever did it kicked Skippy, too. They broke his hip." Tears made her voice ragged, and Luke cursed under his breath, enraged at whoever would do such things.

"Morgan's at the hospital," Tess went on. "She said I shouldn't stay here alone." Her voice was hesitant. "I know it's late and everything, but could I come and spend the rest of the night with Sophie?''

''Absolutely. Stay right where you are—I'm coming to get you. I'm leaving right now.'' He took the stairs two at a time, the puppy in his arms. He awakened Sophie gently and put the furry little dog on the bed beside her. ''This is William, sweetheart. He's yours, and I'm afraid you're going to have to baby-sit him for a while.'' He told her quickly what had happened, asking that she prepare the spare room for Tessa.

He'd pick the girl up and bring her here, but then he was heading down to St. Joe's. The girls would be fine on their own, but he needed to be with the woman he loved.

SHE'D NEVER FELT more alone. Morgan poured herself a cup of the dubious coffee from the pot in the staff lounge on ICU.

It was after one in the morning. India had stabilized and been transferred up here, and Morgan stayed beside her as the nurses settled her amidst the complex machines that monitored every heartbeat, every breath. Morgan had talked to her mother, a steady stream of encouragement, but she wasn't sure India had even heard her.

A strong hand on her shoulder startled her,

and she jumped and slopped her coffee on the carpet.

"Luke!" All at once she knew that it was him she'd longed for since this nightmare began. Hands shaking, she set the coffee cup on the table and moved into his waiting arms with a cry of relief. "Oh, Luke, thank you for coming. Is Tessa okay?"

"Safe at home with Sophie. They were making hot chocolate when I left. They both said to give you their love." He held her close, and she could smell cold night air on his jacket.

"How's India?"

She outlined the situation in a few tense sentences, adding, "They couldn't sustain her blood pressure. Her heart stopped about twenty minutes ago. They gave her intracardiac epinephrine and used the paddles to start it again, but it doesn't look too good."

Morgan's voice quavered, and for a moment she was unable to go on. She leaned into him, his arms a welcome bulwark against all the confusing things that had happened to her this night. She laid her head on his chest and closed her eyes for a moment, aware of the tension, the fierce and frightening emotions that she was suppressing. Aware, too, that the comfort he was offering was temporary.

"She's stable now?" His voice rumbled in his chest, right against her ear.

Morgan shrugged with weary resignation. "For the moment. She's very weak. Her heart condition is quite advanced."

"Why don't you lie down for a while? I'll be here, and I'll wake you if there's any change."

She shook her head. "I can't. I feel as if I've had too much coffee—every nerve is doing a tap dance." The smile she attempted was wobbly.

"Sit, at least." He propelled her over to the couch, and she sank down beside him, his arm still holding her close against his side. He didn't ask questions about the break-in. He didn't mention their last meeting, either, or the things she'd said, and Morgan was thankful. All she could think of right at this moment was India and her own negligence.

Somehow Luke sensed it. "You had no way of knowing about your mother's heart, Morgan."

But his quiet reassurance incensed her, and she threw off his arm and sprang to her feet. "That's garbage and you know it! I saw her every day. I should have noticed. I'm supposed to be a doctor, for crying out loud!" She slammed her palms against her thighs, frustration almost choking her. "I keep asking myself how I could have lived with her all this time and not even noticed what was happening.''

The words spilled from her mouth, and the anger she felt at herself was like a burning sickness in her chest. ''When they took her clothing off I couldn't believe how thin she is, Luke, how fragile. Skin and bone. I should have noticed that, at least. I felt like an idiot down in the ER.''

Luke was watching her and frowning. ''Stop it, Morgan. It's not your fault any of this happened. You know as well as I do that if patients want to hide symptoms, they can. We're not magicians. She should have told you she was ill.''

He was saying the right things, but they didn't ease the guilt that ate at her. Nothing did, not his arms or his words, and she couldn't even stand still, she was so agitated. She stalked across the room, back and forth, her arms clasped across her middle, trying to ease the sickness in her gut.

''That's not all, either. I'm pretty sure it was Dylan who broke into the house tonight. I think Tessa's been seeing him again without telling me.'' She explained about the key and India's fur coats and jewelry. ''He's the only one who could have known about all that. Oh, Luke, I feel like such a total failure in every way.''

The laugh she tried for failed. ''There I was, telling you what you were doing wrong with Sophie, and my own family is falling apart around my ears. Tessa told me tonight she wants to move out. India didn't even tell me she was sick or that she'd sold her trailer in Florida and planned to move in with me."

She was becoming more and more upset. "Then this thing with Dylan. It makes me so...so..." She borrowed one of his favorite oaths. "So *bloody* mad." She was trembling. "And worst of all, there's you. I miss being with you so much."

She shook her head, and utter misery overwhelmed her.

"I just don't know what to do, Luke. I feel as if I'm about to fly apart, and I'm so terribly ashamed of myself."

Luke got to his feet and took her hand, tugging her toward the door. "Come. Come with me. There's something I want to show you."

She objected, but he half pulled her down the corridor to the elevator, not answering her questions about where they were going.

He got off on the maternity ward and led her like a child down the quiet corridor. The nurse at the station looked up, recognized them and went back to her charts.

Luke opened the door to the newborn nursery. He bent over the first bassinet he came to, deftly scooped the sleeping baby out and gently placed it in Morgan's arms.

CHAPTER EIGHTEEN

CONFUSED, SHE automatically accepted the blanket-wrapped bundle, cradling it against her and frowning up at him. "I don't get it, Luke. Whose baby is this? What's going on?"

He crossed his arms on his chest and leaned back against the wall. "I learned this when I was a student. The nursing matron on Maternity was a regular battle-ax. She had all of us interns intimidated, although we pretended otherwise. One night she was giving one of the other fellows holy hell over some breach of her rule book, and he broke down in front of her and cried. It turned out his wife had left him that day for another man.

"Matron never said another word, just hustled him into the newborn nursery and plunked a baby in his arms and ordered him to stay there and hold it until he felt better. He told me afterward that it worked—it put everything back into perspective for him. I still do it myself when I get desperate. I sneak up here and just hold a baby for a while." He smiled at her, his eyes filled with such kindness and compassion her heart seemed to melt.

"It always makes me feel better. Babies are very calming, and I need to be able to talk to you without having you run off on me."

Morgan looked down into the flower face of the child in her arms. The baby yawned and stretched, banging a minuscule hand against her chest. In spite of herself, she smiled, and with the smile came the release of the tears she'd been using ferocious anger to avoid.

She sniffed once and then again, but they poured down her cheeks in a torrent, and Luke took a handful of tissues from a nearby cart and gently dabbed first at her face, then at the baby's. "We don't want to drown the poor wee fellow," he teased gently. He fished another tissue out of the box and held it to her nose. "Blow," he ordered.

She did, and in companionable silence, they stood for a while, Luke lounging against the wall, Morgan unconsciously rocking the baby.

"I'm in love with you, Morgan." His words were soft and low, so unexpected she almost dropped the bundle she held. She opened her mouth to say she loved him, too, but he held up a cautionary hand. "I'm in love with you, but I can't promise you more than that, not yet. I want to ask you to marry me, but the timing is all wrong.''

She swallowed hard and waited, speechless for once, and he sighed and rubbed his eyes and then gave her a sad, crooked smile. ''You have serious problems to work out with Tessa and your mother, and I have a lot of work to do in the coming months to get to know my daughter. I've begun, but it's going to take time and energy. I'll probably be a grandparent before I've learned how to be a father.''

He moved closer to her, stroking a finger down her cheek, outlining her mouth with his thumb. ''You see, my darling, loving is easy for you, but I'm just beginning to realize how hard it is for me to trust, or to accept love and give it freely. The things you said to me before you walked out the other night made me angry, and they hurt like hell, but they needed saying.''

She started to apologize for hurting him, but he shook his head and grimaced. ''They were all true. I've pretty much ignored Sophie since my wife's death, and when she became pregnant, I handled the whole thing as badly as possible.''

Morgan leaped to his defense. ''But it must have been awful for you, losing your wife.'' She didn't realize how wistful her voice sounded. ''Sophie's told me how much you loved her, how happy you all were together.''

"I'm glad Sophie remembers it that way." He shook his head. "It's not the way it was, though." He told her about Deborah. "The marriage I believed to be reasonably good had broken down, and I hadn't even noticed."

Morgan's face registered the shock she felt. How could any woman married to Luke even consider another man?

"I raged and blamed her," he went on. "I was angry and bitter for a long time, and when I got beyond that and took a look at myself, I began to doubt I could ever sustain any sort of love relationship. Certainly I'd failed with marriage, and with Sophie. It wasn't until I made love to you that first time that I began to see what had been missing in my marriage, why I'd put my energy and most of my time into my work. The feelings I had for you scared the hell out of me, because I'd never felt anything remotely like them before."

"Me, either." Morgan's heart swelled with love for him.

"I don't know what the future will bring, but if you're willing, I want to start over, Morgan. I want you and me to be part of each other's families this time. I'd like to get to know Tessa. I want you to be Sophie's friend, and meet Jason and his family. I'd like to help you any way I can with your mother."

It was what she'd longed for, but when she thought of Tessa and Dylan and India, she knew it wasn't going to be easy.

"You sure you know what you're getting into?" She was teasing him, but she was warning him, too. She was also trying to figure out what else this new beginning might involve. "Luke." She felt her face getting warm, and she bent her head over the baby, feeling the blush rise to her hairline. "What about the houseboat?"

He tipped her chin up so he could look at her. His green eyes twinkled, and this time his smile was wide. "I think we deserve one little secret, don't you?" He leaned over the baby to kiss her.

After a while Morgan drew away long enough to lay the warm bundle back in the bassinet. The baby had helped, but knowing Luke loved her was what had eased the heartache. Her anger was gone, and she felt a new sense of hope and optimism as they went hand in hand back down to ICU.

They stayed at St. Joe's another hour, and when it seemed that India's condition would remain relatively stable, Luke drove Morgan home through the deserted streets of the city. Morgan saw everything through a blurry fog of weariness. It had been a long and difficult night, and it wasn't over yet. She still had to talk to Tessa and decide what to do about her suspicions about Dylan Vogler.

She fell asleep on Luke's shoulder before they'd gone many blocks, waking when the car stopped in front of his house.

Sophie and Tessa must have been watching for them. They were waiting in the entrance hall, still in pajamas.

"How's India? Is...is she gonna be all right?" Tessa's face was pinched and white, and it was obvious Sophie had been crying.

"Is she gonna die?" Sophie's mouth trembled, and Luke put an arm around each girl as Morgan did her best to explain India's condition.

"No one knows for certain if she'll come through this." She steeled herself to tell them what she knew to be true. "Even if she does, she won't have very long. Her heart is wearing out. She must have been sick for a long time, and hitting her head the way she did has been very hard on her."

The girls exchanged glances.

"There's something we've gotta tell you, and it's real hard to say," Tessa burst out, twisting out from under Luke's arm and moving away from them.

Sophie swallowed hard and turned agonized gray eyes up to her father. "It's our fault India got hurt, Daddy."

"What do you mean?" Luke frowned at her.

Tessa wrapped her arms around her thin torso. Morgan could see that she was trembling. "It wasn't Sophie, it was me. She only came along because I kept naggin' her." In a gush of words, she told them about skipping the Monday meeting and going to meet Dylan and Brody. "I bragged to them about India's stuff—the jewelry and fur coats and things. I was..." She gulped and stared up at the ceiling. "I was a little drunk. Dylan had some vodka."

She saw the horror on Luke's face and hurriedly added, "Sophie didn't have a drop, just me. I even told them we were gonna be at the play. I said all of us were going. And Dylan knew about the key in the backyard—I used it once when he was with me." Her troubled gaze met Morgan's. "You figured that out. And Sophie and I both know for sure it was them that did it. But it wasn't Sophie's fault, it was mine." Her tone was vehement.

Sophie shook her head impatiently. "I told you before, Tessa, I've got a brain. I can think for myself. You didn't tie me up and drag me along. I'm just as much to blame as you. I...I wanted to make Jason jealous, and I was really mad at Daddy." Her gaze skittered to her father's face, and despite her brave words, Morgan saw the apprehension in her eyes.

Luke was staring down at her, and it was impossible to tell from his expression what he was feeling or how he was going to react.

Morgan could feel every nerve in her body tense. Only hours ago, Luke had said he wanted them to share their problems. He loved her, she knew deep in her soul that he did, but that was the easy part. This was where things became much more difficult, this would be an indication whether or not they could ever truly be a family.

Everything in her seemed to stop for a moment, waiting for the rest of her life to take shape.

THE ROOM WAS very still all of a sudden.

Luke's first reaction was anger, swift and familiar, burning like a fiery chain that twisted itself around his chest. The very thought of Sophie being with Dylan and that other thug, Brody, made him tremble with rage.

She'd lied to him just when he was trying to learn to trust her. He despised being lied to. He'd known all along Tessa was a bad influence. He should never have allowed...

He looked up and saw Morgan watching him. He looked at Tessa, and then at Sophie, and he saw the expressions on their young faces.

All of a sudden, something inside of him ground to a halt. Everything he wanted was in this room. The key to happiness was here, and it was his to turn. He could open the door wide or lock it forever. The choice was his.

He drew in a deep, cleansing breath that hurt his ribs, but the second was easier. His voice wasn't normal, but it was the best he could manage.

"It sounds to me as if you and Tessa made a bad error in judgment, Soph, but everyone does that sometimes." He drew the girls to him, one under each arm. "Let's go make Morgan some breakfast, and we'll all talk this over and figure out what we should do."

Luke turned and looked at Morgan.

Through the blurring of her tears she knew she'd love this man for always.

CHAPTER NINETEEN

ST. JOE'S MEDICAL CENTER was sorta like an ancient castle, Tessa decided as she hurried through the complex maze of winding corridors that led to the medical ward. The sports bag she was carrying got heavier with every step, and it was a relief to finally step into the small private room. She closed the door behind her and tried to smile.

"Hey, India, how ya doin?" Now that she was here, Tessa felt really nervous. It had been eight days since India was hurt, and although she'd visited her every one of those days, this was the first time Tessa had been really alone with the old woman. It was India's first day out of the intensive care ward, and there wasn't exactly a lot of privacy up there.

"Boy, look at all the flowers." The room was filled with bouquets of every sort. Doc Gilbert had brought the red long-stemmed roses, and on the bedside table was the cute teddy bear Sophie had left.

Tess approached the bed, hefting the sports bag carefully onto the armchair beside it.

"Hello, young lady." India's voice was sort of a sigh. She had oxygen prongs in her nose, and it was still a shock to see how puffy she'd gotten and how blue her skin was, particularly around her nose. She smiled at Tessa, though, and Tess leaned close to hear what she was saying.

"What have you got in your bag for me? The food here is disgusting." India complained steadily about the hospital food, even though she hardly took two bites of anything.

She was a world-class complainer, no doubt about that. Tessa had made a habit of bringing in little treats for her—cookies she'd baked, or a taste of whatever she and Morgan had made for dinner the previous day.

"You're not gonna believe what I brought you today. You gotta close your eyes."

"Humph." India managed to look offended, but she did as she was told, and Tessa grinned as she reached into the bag and carefully lifted Skippy out and laid him on the bed beside India. "I was scared he'd take a fit in the hall and get us both kicked out. If somebody comes in, hide him under the covers."

"Skippy! Oh, you brought me Skippy." The way India said it made Tess really glad she'd gone to the trouble of smuggling the little dog in. India's eyes got all teary, and her face sort of crumpled as she stroked Skippy's black fur with a trembling hand.

"The vet put that cast on his hip. He figgers he'll be as good as new in a coupla weeks," Tess gabbled. It was so hard, trying to talk normally to somebody who was gonna die, maybe even today. And what made it worse was that India couldn't talk much; she just didn't have enough breath for it.

Morgan had explained what was happening to her, the way her heart was like a pump that had worn out and how all this gunk had backed up into India's lungs so that breathing got harder and harder. Morgan had said that all the medicine had stopped working now; there wasn't anything more doctors could really do. There were already scary moments when India didn't take a breath for such a long time Tessa's own chest hurt with waiting.

Morgan had asked if India wanted to come home, but the old lady absolutely refused. She said she liked it here, and Tess could see why. All the staff fussed over her because they knew she was Morgan's mother. And India took full advantage, pressing the call button for the slightest little thing. The nurses didn't seem to care, though. They spoiled her silly, and everybody pretended she was getting better.

Tessa thought of what she'd come here to say.

"Yesterday the cops caught the guys who

knocked ya down and took your stuff, India. They found your fur coat and some of your jewelry, too.''

''About time.'' India looked pleased.

Tessa's heart was hammering.

This was really tough. Morgan had said it was up to her whether or not to tell India the full story about Dylan and Brody, about her part in the whole awful mess. And even Frannie had said that it wasn't really necessary, that going to the police and telling the truth was the important part, but Tessa knew this was something she had to do.

''One of those guys who hurt you was my boyfriend,'' she began, and she couldn't even look at the old woman as she stumbled through her confession. Skippy whined once or twice, and India soothed him with her hand, but she didn't try to interrupt.

''It was awful of me to tell them about you and your stuff, and even before that I wasn't very nice to ya, and I'm real sorry about that.'' Tessa's hands were all sweaty, and she wiped them down her jeans. ''I just wanted ya to know,'' she finished lamely, daring to glance at India. If the old lady was feeling better, Tessa figured she'd really let loose at her now, the way she had so many times before. In fact, Tessa wished with all her heart that India *could* just sit up and blast her good.

"I'll understand if ya don't want me to come up here anymore," Tessa went on. "But when you..." Her voice faltered. "When you come home again, I promise I'll try to be lots nicer than I was before."

It wasn't going to happen, but Tess didn't know what else to say. She waited in agony for India's response.

"Nonsense."

Tess thought she must have misunderstood. She leaned closer to India. "Sorry. What did ya say?"

"Nonsense." India puffed at the oxygen and glared up at Tessa. "Women are much more interesting when they're not nice." Again she sucked in oxygen. "Don't you forget it." Her swollen hand was stroking Skippy's back. Her eyes seemed to have sunk into the puffiness of her face, but Tessa could have sworn she winked.

"I like you as you are, did from the start. Got spunk, like me. And when I come home," she puffed, "I want your bedroom. Mine..." She had to stop again, struggling for air, and the seconds ticked by and she didn't breathe and didn't breathe, and then finally she did again.

"Mine is far too small," she added with a wicked grin.

CHAPTER TWENTY

IT WAS THREE-FIFTEEN in the morning in the small labor room, and the intervals between Sophie's contractions had dramatically shortened. Morgan snapped off the glove she'd worn for the examination.

"Not much longer now, sweetie. This is the last part of your labor and you're just doing a first-class job. You're already six centimeters dilated, so we'll be going to the delivery room real soon now."

She used a washcloth to tenderly smooth the girl's sweaty face. The monitor showed the baby was fine, and apart from a slight elevation in Sophie's blood pressure, things were going exceptionally well.

Life was good, Morgan thought exultantly, snapping off her other glove.

Apart from India's death just before Christmas, the past few months had been the happiest she'd ever known, although losing her mother had been exceptionally hard for her. Only in the last few days of India's life had she confessed how much she loved her daughter, and how proud she was of her. Morgan had longed for more time, so they could get to know each other in a way they never had.

Luke had proposed on Christmas Eve, on bended knee, with Tessa and Sophie as tearful witnesses. They'd marry in June, and then they hoped to have a baby of their own as soon as possible.

The girls found it hilarious that Sophie's child might soon have aunts and uncles younger than himself.

Sophie's pregnancy had been wonderfully normal, without even the ordinary annoying problems expectant mothers usually had, and her labor was progressing as easily as labor ever did. She began a strong contraction, and Morgan helped her through it, rubbing her back and coaching her breathing.

When it was over, Morgan said, "I'll get your dad and Jason in here and tell them we're gonna have a baby real soon."

She moved toward the door.

"Morgan?" There was something in Sophie's voice that made Morgan stop and quickly move back to the bed.

"Morgan, my eyes are funny. Everything's all blurry. And...I can't...get my breath..."

Before the sentence was complete, Sophie's eyes rolled back in her head, and to Morgan's absolute horror, she went into seizure, her swollen body bucking, her limbs thrashing uncontrollably. The monitor that signaled the baby's heartbeat went suddenly flat.

Eclampsia. The terrible word shot through Morgan's brain like an electric shock. *Sudden elevated blood pressure, followed by convulsive seizures, coma...often fatal for both mother and child.*

Fear, stark and vivid, slammed through her. She grabbed a washcloth and forced a wad of it between Sophie's teeth, and at the same time restrained the girl so she wouldn't throw herself off the narrow bed.

"Juliet!" Morgan screamed for the nurse and hit the emergency call button, and in seconds the room was overflowing with people.

"Call a code, we've got to section her. Let's get her up to the OR."

Morgan caught a glimpse of the horror on Luke's white face, knowing it was a reflection of her own. It seemed unthinkable, but both of them knew they could easily lose Sophie and her baby in the next few minutes.

For an instant, she was immobilized by panic. In the blink of an eye, she saw their happiness, their future, scarred beyond redemption by awful tragedy. And then, between one breath and the next, years of experience clicked in. She was only an obstetrician dealing with a difficult case.

The well-being of the girl on the table was the only thing that mattered.

Her commands were urgent but calm. "Get that portable oxygen in here. Let's get her on the elevator, load the equipment on the bed. Move it—"

They all went hurtling down the corridor, maneuvering the bed onto the elevator, bodies squeezed against bodies, the air redolent with tension. Jason was ordered to stay behind, but Morgan knew that Luke was close by. The door closed, the elevator began to rise, voices echoed in the cramped space.

"She's fully dilated—she mustn't push." Morgan's deep voice penetrated the hubbub. "Sophie, can you hear me? Don't push, please don't push."

But Morgan's frantic command went unheeded. Sophie's body had relaxed, the seizure over for the moment, but she was only half awake, not responding.

Morgan crouched at the end of the bed, supporting Sophie's legs on her shoulders.

"Sophie, don't push." Juliet, too, was bent over Sophie, frantically repeating the command into her ear, but Sophie strained and groaned.

"This baby's crowning. She's going to deliver...."

Dark, matted swirls of hair and the top of a tiny head became visible, and then Sophie screamed, the sound deafening in the cramped space.

The tiny skull emerged from Sophie's body, and Morgan supported it. "Sophie, wait. Don't push now until I say so," she begged. "Please, honey, don't push..." Slowly, the head rotated. A shoulder emerged.

Sophie screamed again, the sound dwindling into a moan, and then another convulsion seized her, her entire body alternately thrashing and bearing down uncontrollably.

The elevator jerked to a stop.

A small totally white body, limp and still and streaked with blood, shot into Morgan's hands. Luke's grandson, a fine big boy, and he was flat, showing no visible signs of life.

Help me here, please, God...

After an eon, the elevator door sighed open, and everyone exploded into the hall, running hard, bursting through the doors to the OR.

"Call a code 333..." *Baby in serious trouble.*

The next few seconds were a blur of activity.

Resuscitation was begun. Intertracheal tubes were swiftly put into place to deliver oxygen to the baby and Sophie. A neonatal team worked frantically over the small, still child.

Morgan, desperately tending to Sophie, administered Valium, magnesium sulfate, phenobarbital. Dilantin, to halt the seizures. All the while she felt as if parts of her were also watching the concentrated activity surrounding the child, watching Luke, standing helplessly by while she lost his daughter, his grandson.

Memories of Tessa's baby stabbed through Morgan's mind.

Please, not again. We need a miracle here...

Relief hit her like a wave when Sophie sighed and opened her eyes, but then Morgan heard the quiet, desperate note in the voice of the specialist working on her son.

"Apgar 0." They'd lost the baby.

And then, an instant later, quiet jubilation.

"He's breathing on his own. He's pinking up."

"Apgar 5."

A small, husky cry sounded, the sweetest music Morgan had ever heard. A jubilant cheer went up from the team of specialists.

"Apgar 9."

Thank you, angels. Sophie and her son had survived.

Morgan lifted her head and searched for Luke. Through the tears blurring her vision, she looked into his anguished gaze. She grinned behind her mask and lifted both thumbs in the age-old sign for victory.

Darn it all, they'd have their happily ever after, she and this man she loved.

They'd earned it.

Late that evening, Morgan yawned and flexed

her aching shoulders as she made her way to the case room where Sophie was still being closely monitored.

Both Morgan and Luke had been in and out of the crowded room every few hours all day, delighted and relieved that things were staying absolutely normal with both mother and son. Jason and his family had also been there much of the day, and Tessa, of course, all of them vying to hold the baby.

Morgan hadn't yet had a chance to just sit and enjoy him herself, and she was pretty sure Luke hadn't, either.

After Sophie's early-morning crisis, Morgan had been called to a second delivery, and then one of Luke's patients also went into labor. After that things were crazy on the maternity floor. Between the two of them, they'd delivered five babies today, as well as Sophie's son.

Morgan was both exhausted and exultant over the new lives she'd helped bring into the world. Miracles, all of them, but why did they all have to arrive on this particular day?

Maybe it was the phase of the moon, she mused, yawning again, or perhaps it was just the glorious spring sunshine that made babies decide to come in batches. Whatever it was, she hoped the rush was over, for her sake and for Luke's.

She opened the door to Sophie's room. Only the night-light was on, and a doting grandfather sprawled in a chair, cradling a blanket-wrapped bundle beside the bed of his sleeping daughter.

"I thought I might find you here," Morgan whispered, automatically checking the blood pressure cuff attached to Sophie's arm, pleased with what she saw.

The danger was really over. With a sigh of relief, she looped an arm around Luke's neck, rested her chin on his thick dark hair and bent over to look at the baby.

The tiny boy wasn't asleep. His deep blue eyes were wide open, and one curled-up leg poked out of the wrappings and rested against Luke's chest. He looked up at them, his brow furrowed as if he were pondering their place in his new life.

"He's absolutely beautiful. He's got your hair." Morgan stroked the little head with its halo of black silk and held out her arms. "Here, give him to me. You've had your turn."

Luke handed over the fragrant bundle.

Morgan's heart swelled with love for this child whose arrival had been so precarious. "Does he have a name yet?"

"Duncan."

She studied the little face and nodded. "It suits him. He's going to be a big, strong man. Drop-dead handsome, like his grampa."

"I suppose I'll get used to it, but this grampa thing is making me feel elderly." Luke gently took the baby from Morgan's arms. "Duncan, let's take you back to the nursery." He bent his head so that his lips were close to her ear. "Then, Doctor, I don't suppose you'd care to pay a visit to this houseboat I know of and help an old man regain his youth?"

She grinned up at him wickedly. She didn't feel the least bit tired anymore. "Would that be called a labor of love, Doctor?"

He pressed a kiss to her lips. "Most definitely."

She pretended to sigh. "Then in the interests of medicine, I suppose I could be persuaded."

EVER HAD ONE OF THOSE DAYS?

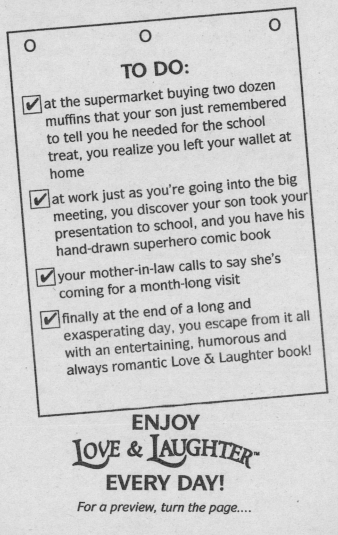

TO DO:

- ✔ at the supermarket buying two dozen muffins that your son just remembered to tell you he needed for the school treat, you realize you left your wallet at home

- ✔ at work just as you're going into the big meeting, you discover your son took your presentation to school, and you have his hand-drawn superhero comic book

- ✔ your mother-in-law calls to say she's coming for a month-long visit

- ✔ finally at the end of a long and exasperating day, you escape from it all with an entertaining, humorous and always romantic Love & Laughter book!

ENJOY
LOVE & LAUGHTER™
EVERY DAY!

For a preview, turn the page....

*Here's a sneak peek at
Carrie Alexander's THE AMOROUS HEIRESS
Available September 1997...*

"YOU'RE A VERY popular lady," Jed Kelley observed as Augustina closed the door on her suitors.

She waved a hand. "Just two of a dozen." Technically true since her grandmother had put her on the open market. "You're not afraid of a little competition, are you?"

"Competition?" He looked puzzled. "I thought the position was mine."

Augustina shook her head, smiling coyly. "You didn't think Grandmother was the final arbiter of the decision, did you? I say a trial period is in order." No matter that Jed Kelley had miraculously passed Grandmother's muster, Augustina felt the need for a little propriety. But, on the other hand, she could be married before the summer was out and be free as a bird, with the added bonus of a husband it wouldn't be all that difficult to learn to love.

She got up the courage to reach for his hand,

and then just like that, she—Miss Gussy Gutless Fairchild—was holding Jed Kelley's hand. He looked down at their linked hands. "Of course, you don't really know what sort of work I can do, do you?"

A funny way to put it, she thought absently, cradling his callused hand between both of her own. "We can get to know each other, and then, if that works out..." she murmured. *Wow.* If she'd known what this arranged marriage thing was all about, she'd have been a supporter of Grandmother's campaign from the start!

"Are you a palm reader?" Jed asked gruffly. His voice was as raspy as sandpaper and it was rubbing her all the right ways, but the question flustered her. She dropped his hand.

"I'm sorry."

"No problem," he said, "as long as I'm hired."

"Hired!" she scoffed. "What a way of putting it!"

Jed folded his arms across his chest. "So we're back to the trial period."

"Yes." Augustina frowned and her gaze dropped to his work boots. Okay, so he wasn't as well off as the majority of her suitors, but really, did he think she was going to *pay* him to marry her?

"Fine, then." He flipped her a wave and, speechless, she watched him leave. She was trembling all over like a malaria victim in a snowstorm, shot with hot charges and cold shivers until her brain was numb. This couldn't be true. Fantasy men didn't happen to nice girls like her.

"Augustina?"

Her grandmother's voice intruded on Gussy's privacy. "Ahh. There you are. I see you met the new gardener?"

HARLEQUIN AND SILHOUETTE
ARE PLEASED TO PRESENT

Love, marriage—and the pursuit of family!

Check your retail shelves for these upcoming titles:

July 1997
Last Chance Cafe by Curtiss Ann Matlock
The most determined bachelor in Oklahoma is in trouble! A
lovely widow with three daughters has moved next door—and
the girls want a dad! But he wants to know if their mom needs
a husband....

August 1997
Thorne's Wife by Joan Hohl

Pennsylvania. It was only to be a marriage of convenience—
until they fell in love! Now, three years later, tragedy
threatens to separate them forever and Valerie wants only to
be in the strength of her husband's arms. For she has some
very special news for the expectant father...

September 1997
Desperate Measures by Paula Detmer Riggs
New Mexico judge Amanda Wainwright's daughter has been
kidnapped, and the price of her freedom is a verdict in
favor of a notorious crime boss. So enters ex-FBI agent
Devlin Buchanan—ruthless, unstoppable—and soon there is
no risk he will not take for her.

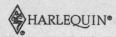

HARLEQUIN WOMEN
KNOW ROMANCE
WHEN THEY SEE IT.

And they'll see it on **ROMANCE CLASSICS**, the new 24-hour TV channel devoted to romantic movies and original programs like the special **Romantically Speaking-Harlequin® Goes Prime Time.**

Romantically Speaking-Harlequin® Goes Prime Time introduces you to many of your favorite romance authors in a program developed exclusively for Harlequin® readers.

Watch for **Romantically Speaking-Harlequin® Goes Prime Time** beginning in the summer of 1997.

If you're not receiving ROMANCE CLASSICS, call your local cable operator or satellite provider and ask for it today!

Escape to the network of your dreams.

ROMANCE CLASSICS

HARLEQUIN SUPERROMANCE®

There's more to the story...

For the very first time, award-winning authors

Leigh Greenwood
and
Peg Sutherland

have combined their unique talents
in a saga that spans two generations.

An unforgettable tale that proves once again
that true love really does conquer all!

Join us in the Old South for this outstanding story
of pride and passion!

ONLY YOU (#754)

Coming in September 1997

Look for *Only You* wherever Harlequin books are sold.

Let's Celebrate!

LOVE & LAUGHTER™

invites you to
the party of the season!

Grab your popcorn and be prepared to laugh as we celebrate with **LOVE & LAUGHTER**.

Harlequin's newest series is going Hollywood!

Let us make you laugh with three months of terrific books, authors and romance, plus a chance to win a FREE 15-copy video collection of the best romantic comedies ever made.

For more details look in the back pages of any Love & Laughter title, from July to September, at your favorite retail outlet.

Don't forget the popcorn!

Available wherever
Harlequin books are sold.

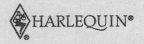

◈ HARLEQUIN®

Look us up on-line at: http://www.romance.net

LLCELEB